FRAIL SISTER

by Karen Green

siglio 2018 New York

Book and cover design: Karen Green and Natalie Kraft
First Edition
ISBN: 978-1-938221-19-4
Printed and bound in China

siglio uncommon books at the intersection of art & literature
PO Box 111, Catksill, New York 12414 p 310-857-6935
www.sigliopress.com publisher@sigliopress.com

Available to the trade through Artbook.com/D.A.P.
75 Broad Street, Suite 630, New York, NY 10004
Tel: 212-627-1999 Fax: 212-627-9484

For the Smider Sisters
and
L'elk + J

Burning Oil Tank, Oil City, Pa.

JUVENILE
MUSICALE

Beloved Sister,
This lock of hair to you I give
I pray you keep it while you live
If you should hear that I am dead
Remember this grew on my head

PROGRAMME

Music, sphere descended Maid,
Friend of Pleasure, Wisdom's Aid.
-- Collins

I loved thee, and must love thee still,

In m...

Amid...

My fa...

E'er in...

When br...

Life's go...

Thou wer...

Sent fr...

         i in my stockinged feet
can balance on my toes &
this I am encouraged to do
 We are paid for our spec-
   ialties and it buys our
cabbages, egg noodles, gruel
From their iron rings mama
  pulls down the draperies
to fashion our costumes. the
brocade is grimy but the
  sewing hours she sacrifices
eventually become lore. in
    the meantime, in these
mean times, the glass sequin
  catscratch and bleed us as
we sing our hearts out for a
  stew. we two are a Kiddie
   ~~Kabaret~~   KABARET

Mouse sulks on the
davenport, sharpening a
stick. he is not a pretty
child, but you. how ancient
and solemn your profile
above yr decorated body;
  bleached legs poking out
from salvaged tulle,tap
shoes painted matte gold
and bow-tied. I mostly
do as I am told, I hold
your hand offstage and
on. Everyone has lost
their work except us two
so off we trot,   &
home we come with coins.

Mama gathers roots by
the tracks for dyes and
  boils
our costumes on the stove
 on the stove alongside
the cabbage and tongue.

  Tongue is cheap.

Hate to be a bringdown, but we're
hungry. Kid gloves are dead goat
fingers. The pride of our town,
petroleum, is dead dead deader critters.
A tongue sandwich is a dead cow's
dead tongue, with taste buds. I thought
tongue was French for sandwich meat.
To make matters worse, our woolens
are drenched. We did our song and
dance for the oddfellows last night
but they didn't pay up. Pa's gone
down to give them the what for.

**TINY SINGERS AND
DANCERS WIN FIRST
PLACE IN AMATEURS**

Dandelion broth, rag soup. NO
BELLYACHING. NO BELLYACHING* Not
even Hoover stew. Not even tater-
skin sandwiches 'cause we haven't
the bread. Dry bread and dry water
is whatwe'll get if we don't shape
up, we're reminded. Shit on a shingle.
I LIKE POWDERED MILK AND RICE, you
claim, all singsong. I hate you.
I want Toad-in-a-hole, fried in real
butter. I'LL KILL A TOAD AND A COWBIRD,
volunteers our awful brother. Hate
him, too. Hate wet mittens. Hate church,
and the empty grease can on the stove
reminding us of bacon days. I'LL KILL
A GROUNDHOG & A FALCON & A WOODRAT, he
brags now, whacking the table with
his cutlery. Mother says she'll kill
a Mouse if he doesnt shut his trap.

Mama says before we were
born, oil tanks were
struck by lightning and
the creek carried flaming
petroleum right into our
town, deep-frying all the
bad children in their beds.
It can happen again if we ~~do~~
don't shape up and hunt our
daddy like we mean to find
him. ~~Papa didn't come home~~
for supper again.

Miss Connie
(The Fairy who rewards
generous people.)

* * *
* MJG *
* * *

Bouquet de Melodies

Dear Co...

"It was so wonderful, so marvelous, so gorgeous, so divine. . . ." No, I am not trying to sing. I'm just telling you what we (my mother and I) think of the fine program you and your sis... ...er the radio last evening... ...nute of it, for you both... ...n played the violin beaut...

The other... ...a schoolmate of your... ...e talked ...bout you! ... about you ...ere all ni... ...she would ...ry to bring... ...metime. I hope you will com... as I should be delighted to meet you.

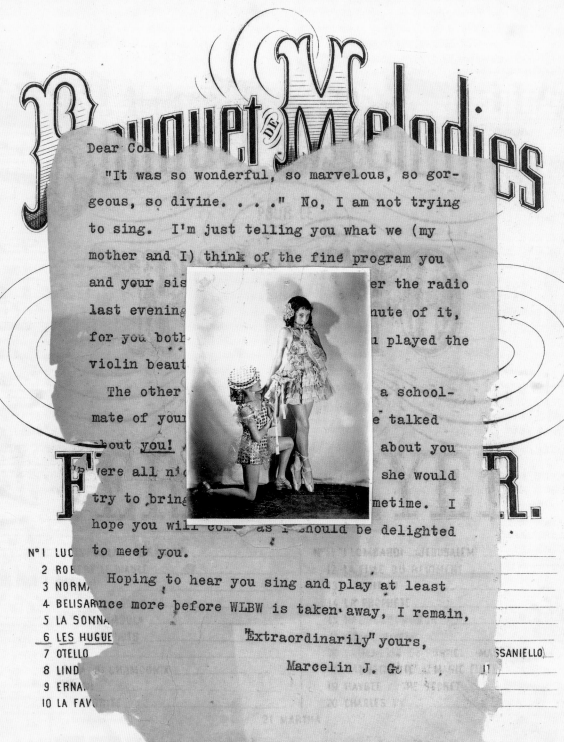

Hoping to hear you sing and play at least ...nce more before WLBW is taken away, I remain,

"Extraordinarily" yours,

Marcelin J. G...

N°1 LUC...
2 ROB...
3 NORM...
4 BELISAR...
5 LA SONN...
6 LES HUGUE...
7 OTELLO
8 LIND...
9 ERNA...
10 LA FAV...

Op 42

PHILADELPHIA   J.E. GOULD
Successor to A.FIOT *Swains Building 164 Chesnut S*ᵗ

OLIVER DITSON
Boston

D.A.TRUAX
Cincinnati

T.S.BERRY
N.York

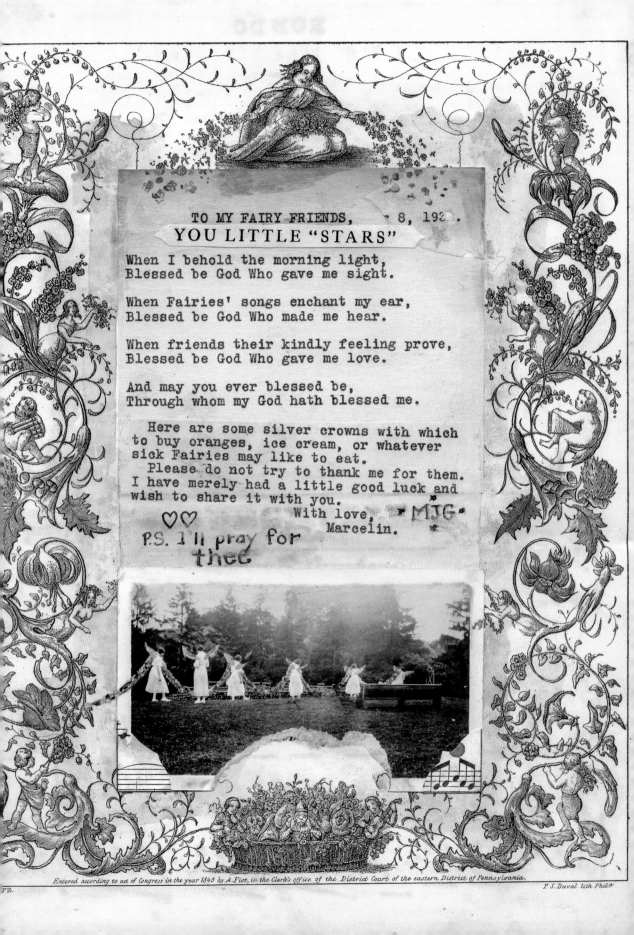

TO MY FAIRY FRIENDS,   8, 19 .

YOU LITTLE "STARS"

When I behold the morning light,
Blessed be God Who gave me sight.

When Fairies' songs enchant my ear,
Blessed be God Who made me hear.

When friends their kindly feeling prove,
Blessed be God Who gave me love.

And may you ever blessed be,
Through whom my God hath blessed me.

Here are some silver crowns with which
to buy oranges, ice cream, or whatever
sick Fairies may like to eat.
Please do not try to thank me for them.
I have merely had a little good luck and
wish to share it with you.

♡♡   With love,   ⋆MJG⋆
                        Marcelin.

P.S. I'll pray for
        thee

That nice cripple has volunteered to
take pictures of our finery and picnic
us as well. That's what Mama calls him,
That Nice Cripple, and that's what she
calls a picnic. He tells me my legs are
meatier than yours, but allows me a chicken
wing from the basket. He tells me my hair
is too dark, even in this afternoon light,
and my nose too long, obscenely French,
possibly Pletzl, "Go sit under the willow."

Your hair is goldenrod and you're an easy
poser, what with that wise face of yours.
You get some kind of cake, too. Frosted.

He ~~jerks~~ jerks and marionettes
around his tripod; violence
happened to his legs so
his elbows are winged for
balance. This is the first of
many afternoons with M.J.G.,
who is also something of a
playwright, we find out:

   I tune in on ~~children's~~ aildren's
programs every Wednesday and
Saturday, and am always glad
when your name, or your sister's, is announced.
   Wishing you both a great
deal of good luck, I shall
now say "Farewell" until
some other time. I'll be
listening!
         Your radio friend,
         Marcelin J. G   .
         (Author of "The Land
         of Lost Children.")

... and a poet!

I would flood your path
       with sunshine,
I would fence you
           from all ill
I would crown you
       with all blessings,
If I could but have
              my will.

(Over.)

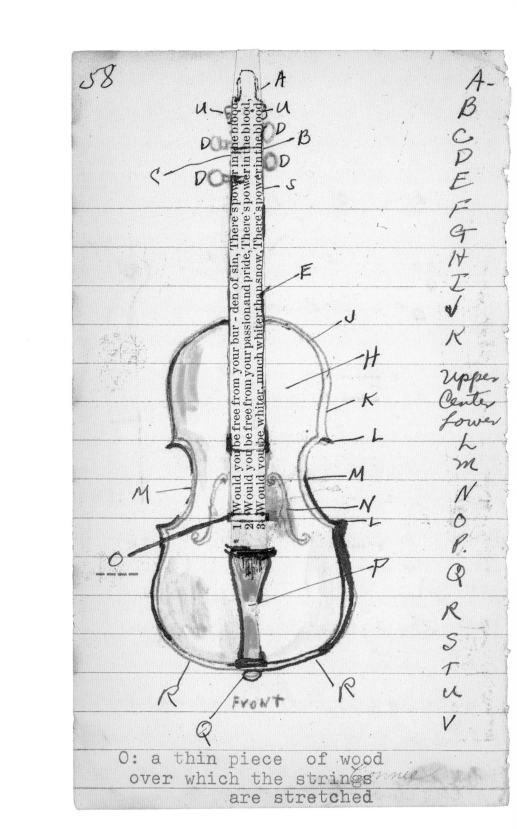

58

O: a thin piece of wood
over which the strings
are stretched

Scroll
Cheeks of the Scroll
Peg Box
Pegs
Fingerboard
Neck
Button
Belly
Back
Purfling
Edges projecting
Over sides (or ribs)
bouts
or middle bouts
bouts
Corners
Center Bout
ff holes
Bridge
Tailpiece
Tailpin
+ rest
Lower bouts
Nut
Shoulder
Eyes of scroll.
Pegs in top +
bottom of
old violins

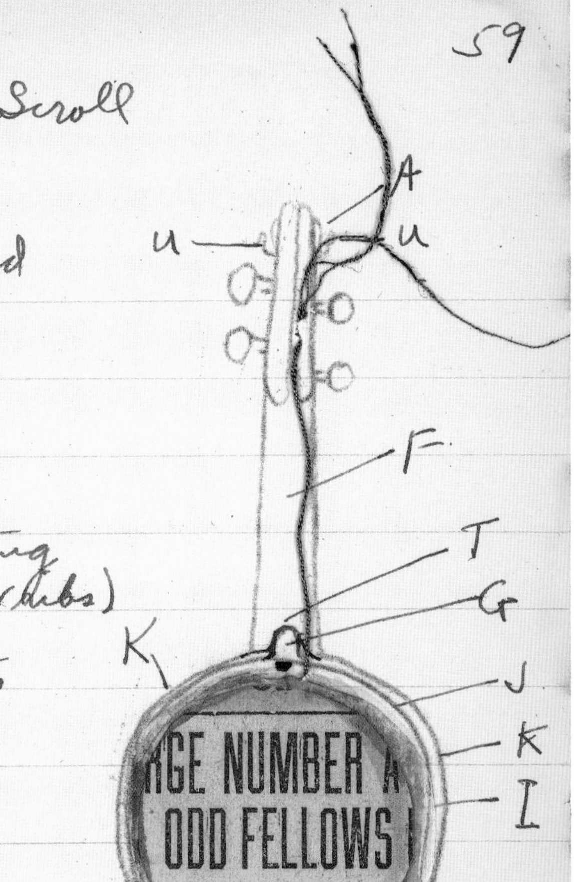

59

            We have our silky tap pants
       on, practicing our triple timestep,
       shaking our fannies. Ma is having
       a Catholic Episode. She tells us
       about the birds and the bees at
       the kitchen table, using you as
       her dummy. X With the watercolors
    Mr. G brought back from Paris, she
       paints a common bird on your tender
    thigh, maybe a wren, then props you
    up and draws a little hornet on the
    other leg. Now sit down, cross your
    legs and make the hornet sting the
       birdie or the bird eat the bug and
    stay this way until matrimony or it's
       brimstone, etcetera for the both
    of you. US.

and I got my mouth washed out with soap.

Sister, You float & I fall

THEODORE PRESSER CO., PHILA., PA.

CLARKE'S MUSIC TABLET

SHORT INTRODUCTORY NUMBER.

OF MASTER OF CEREMONIES.

Not our regular church, but
the castle with sweet smoke
wafting through rainbow windows,
St. Joseph's on Pearl Avenue.
Anyhow,

1   Orchestra Evangelical Church, Garcie Masterson, Conductor.

Harmonica Selection Brother _____ Johnson of Tionesta.

Sisters   Love, I is"

onnie   Song "The Extraordinary Boy"

Xylophone Solo,   ed by Miss Merceded Wei

Quartette   "A   Chas Trax.
        (Chas Tra   h and XXXX Howard Paulson

Sisters   Duet   _Goofus_

s Solo, Harry   s. Trax.

        "T
(Encore) "D

Comedy Dramatic

artette.   Fo

THE BUCKET

Sisters Again. Song and Tap Dance "Over the Viaduct" Comedy

dress – Prof. Chas A. Platt of Grove City College.

Connie Su   – Song –"Mighty Lak a Rose"

tour of   th with   ack Joe"

            Cur

We are not allowed and did we or didn't
we shamefully eat the body of and drink
the blood of because ~~x~~ we were hungry
or curious but mainly rotten to the core.
Mama says Now the WHOLE TOWN KNOWS and
tongues are wagging and what happened to me is
I turned ~~~~ blue from coughing up the
~~biskit~~ bisquit wafer and what happened to
you is you were ~~heled~~ held aloft by Jesus
you claim and floated there above the rectory
steps, higher and blonder. I suggest you
fainted upwards but I am getting the scarlet
fever. At any rate, gravity was ~~supernormally-~~
~~defied by you and now the Ma and Pa fight~~
~~about Good and Evil begins in earnest:~~
~~Depends on who's doing the floating,~~ says Pa,
whether the verdict be saint or witch.
My tummy was full of electricity, you explain,
and my feet full of tingle. ~~~~ You don't
~~even talk like that. Mama adds~~ Both witches
~~and saints get burned alive,~~ but I think
what happened is miracles live in another
world ~~bu~~ and one showed up in ours briefly,
like it took a wrong turn. SEEN BUT NOT HER
~~HEARD from me, on this they do agree, and~~
~~LIE DOWN because tomorrow is prize-winning~~
~~Thursday at the Schubert Club, we've nothing~~
in the ice box. As for you, little sis, you
can join a convent at a later date.

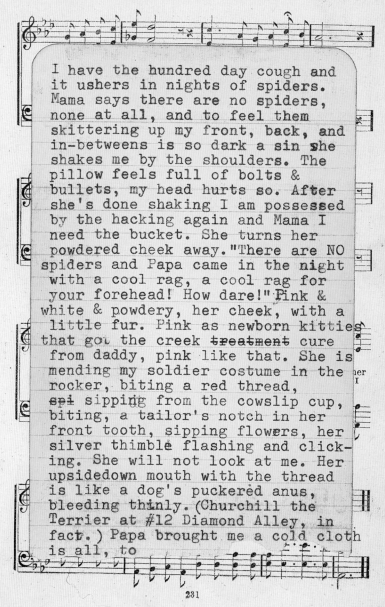

I have the hundred day cough and
it ushers in nights of spiders.
Mama says there are no spiders,
none at all, and to feel them
skittering up my front, back, and
in-betweens is so dark a sin she
shakes me by the shoulders. The
pillow feels full of bolts &
bullets, my head hurts so. After
she's done shaking I am possessed
by the hacking again and Mama I
need the bucket. She turns her
powdered cheek away. "There are NO
spiders and Papa came in the night
with a cool rag, a cool rag for
your forehead! How dare!" Pink &
white & powdery, her cheek, with a
little fur. Pink as newborn kitties
that got the creek ~~treatment~~ cure
from daddy, pink like that. She is
mending my soldier costume in the
rocker, biting a red thread,
~~spi~~ sipping from the cowslip cup,
biting, a tailor's notch in her
front tooth, sipping flowers, her
silver thimble flashing and click-
ing. She will not look at me. Her
upsidedown mouth with the thread
is like a dog's puckered anus,
bleeding thinly. (Churchill the
Terrier at #12 Diamond Alley, in
fact.) Papa brought me a cold cloth
is all, to

COWPER.

Mama the buck

THIS MUSICALE
is presented under the personal dir. of
MRS. H. S. BARLETT
GRADUATE CLARION MUSIC DEPARTMENT
and
Advanced Study at the
OBERLIN CONSERVATORY OF MUSIC

wipe it off. mama the bucket
again, please. bleeding dog
hole and hairy spider legs!
i dont think i said it but
i did and now sour rag soap
my dirty mouth so rotten plums
washed out and ammonia washed out and clotted cream
that butter's gone off, wash
that out too

Stage Furniture Loaned By
C. E. WHITEHILL, KNOX, PA.

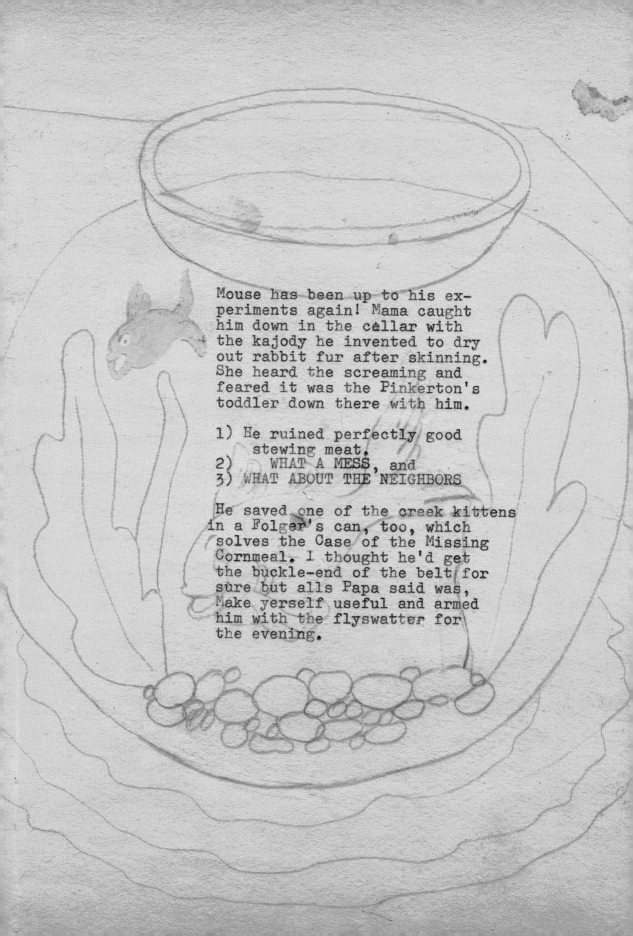

Mouse has been up to his experiments again! Mama caught him down in the cellar with the kajody he invented to dry out rabbit fur after skinning. She heard the screaming and feared it was the Pinkerton's toddler down there with him.

1) He ruined perfectly good stewing meat.
2)   WHAT A MESS, and
3) WHAT ABOUT THE NEIGHBORS

He saved one of the creek kittens in a Folger's can, too, which solves the Case of the Missing Cornmeal. I thought he'd get the buckle-end of the belt for sure but alls Papa said was, Make yerself useful and armed him with the flyswatter for the evening.

NOT A PRETTY CHILD

You were my favorite
You are my favorite
I loved thee, and
must love thee still.

   Our baby brother, Mouse,
was nobody's favorite. I
think it's why he collected
the war souvenirs. Ears and
such.

₮" +⁺9 *!!

Constance

CITIZENSHIP

Habits and Attitudes Desirable for Good Citizenship	REPORTS					
	1	2	3	4	5	6
I. As an Individual—Personal						
1. Has good health habits _____						
2. Obeys promptly and cheerfully _____	X	X	X	X	X	X
3. Does the right thing whether told or not	X	X	X	X	X	X
4. Is careful of						
5. Takes pride i						
6. Calls for help w						
7. Offers helpful sugg						
8. Completes what						
9. Has critical att						
II. As						
1. Cooperates with group in work and play	X	X	X	X	X	X
2. Has self-control_____	X	X	X	X		X X
3. Shows proper consideration for rights of others _____	X	X	X	X	X	X
4. Does his part in keeping school attractive_____						
5. Claims only his share of attention ____						
6. Is courteous to others _____	X	X	X	X	X	X

A cross (X) shows that your cooperation is desired.

FANNY J. CROSBY.   W. H. DOANE.

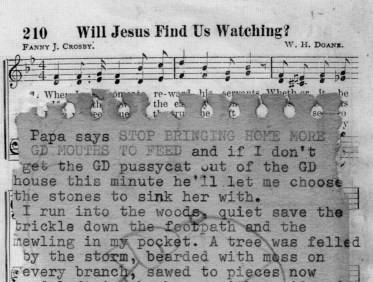

Papa says STOP BRINGING HOME MORE
GD MOUTHS TO FEED and if I don't
get the GD pussycat out of the GD
house this minute he'll let me choose
the stones to sink her with.
I run into the woods, quiet save the
trickle down the footpath and the
mewling in my pocket. A tree was felled
by the storm, bearded with moss on
every branch, sawed to pieces now
and left in chunks on either side of
me. I kneel down to smell the splint-
ered wood, and God is watching me palm
the cat in my pocket, making a bowl
around her so she doesn't get squashed.
The smell blooms all marzipan and
sourgrass, a texture in my nose. The
tree is dead but inside it's sharp
and lively. I imagine the echoing crack
as it toppled, slaughtering a genera-
tion of insects.

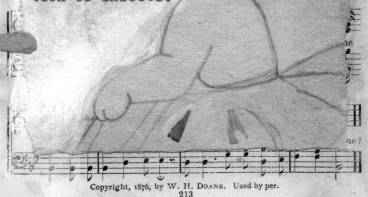

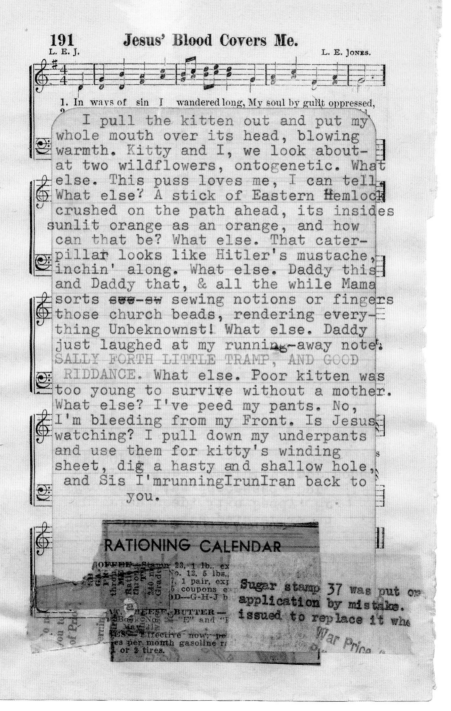

191   **Jesus' Blood Covers Me.**

L. E. J.   L. E. JONES.

1. In ways of sin I wandered long, My soul by guilt oppressed,

I pull the kitten out and put my
whole mouth over its head, blowing
warmth. Kitty and I, we look about—
at two wildflowers, ontogenetic. What
else. This puss loves me, I can tell.
What else? A stick of Eastern Hemlock
crushed on the path ahead, its insides
sunlit orange as an orange, and how
can that be? What else. That cater-
pillar looks like Hitler's mustache,
inchin' along. What else. Daddy this
and Daddy that, & all the while Mama
sorts ~~see-sw~~ sewing notions or fingers
those church beads, rendering everything Unbeknownst! What else. Daddy
just laughed at my running-away note:
SALLY FORTH LITTLE TRAMP, AND GOOD
RIDDANCE. What else. Poor kitten was
too young to survive without a mother.
What else? I've peed my pants. No,
I'm bleeding from my Front. Is Jesus
watching? I pull down my underpants
and use them for kitty's winding
sheet, dig a hasty and shallow hole,
and Sis I'mrunningIrunIran back to
you.

RATIONING CALENDAR

COFFEE—Stamp 23, 1 lb., ex
No. 12, 5 lbs.,
7, 1 pair, exp
5 coupons a
D—G-H-J b

CHEESE, BUTTER—
Book No. 2 "E" and "F
Effective now, pe
es per month gasoline r
1 or 2 tires.

Sugar stamp 37 was put on
application by mistake.
issued to replace it whe

War Price

This hair I give to thee
A token of my love
Remember me or ...

OIL CITY HI

A weak Titusville eleven offered minor opposition as Coach J. J. Connors directed the Oil City High School football team to a 19-6 triumph in the season's opener, thus breaking a victory famine that had extended over a three-year period.

Following this spectacular start, that intangible annoyance known as the "jinx" crept into the intricate joints of what gave promise of developing into a smooth-working gridiron machine, using as its chief weapons injuries, ineligibilities, and disruption within the squad itself. The team promptly went into a nose-dive from which it was never quite able to recover. A list of seven disheartening defeats followed. Notwithstanding the fact that victory had once again taken the shape of an elusive eel, the boys never lost that fighting spirit, and, on the last day of the season, gave probably their best performance of the entire campaign. Despite a snow covered gridiron and a shortage of loyalites present to cheer them on, the Oilers fought the highly favored Farrell Steelers to a virtual standstill, losing by the comparatively small score of 13-0.

Oil City High School Alma Mater

1 Faith have we in Oil City High School we love so well
2 Thee we'll raise in sto-ry and song Oth-er schools a-bove

The rhythm, that he plays puts the cats in
a trance/Nobody there ever bothers to dance/
But when he plays with the bass and guitar/
They holler, Beat me Daddy, eight to the bar

To our knowledge, ours is the first all-girl high school swing band in the country. As we expected, the girls do a lovely job on the sweet music. But to the amazement of most of us they really get "on the beam" in a "jive" number, too. It's a good bet that when these "gals" have been organized a while, they'll lead the boys a merry chase.

Thee we'll cher-ish ev-er more As the years go by.

Under the New Deal,
there are also jobs
for artists at the
camps, what they call
resident artists

IX.

By a Meadow Brook.

According to Mr. G., back before Seneca drilled the first
well here, the Romans used oil
to cure leposy. Leprosy is
punishment for vanity. President
Roosevelt has sent us the CCC
to tidy up the Allegheny forest
and when they've packed up and
gone there will be miles of fresh
nooks for ~~this~~ tripod set-ups.
I wish I could clear hedgerows
for 36 buckaroos a month but
Marcelin says it's work not
meant for ladies and to stay
away from the camps, all them
dirty boys come from kin on
relief. Guttersnipes. Lagerhead
Quinlivens. Trash. His photos
will make us Broadway stars or
wives of great men etc., but I've
bloomed a figure and with it
comes new ways of thinking. My
brain's gone all curvy so I filch
some ink from MJG and make my way
out to Camp Pebble Dell.

I'll get the paddle for painting *resident artist* on my violin case later, but meanwhile I set myself up on a nice, flat stump and straightaway start inking what I reckon are the Boys' sleeping quarters. I'm not half bad. And that's where I meet Erastus, who scares the living daylights sneaking up behind me like that and first thing says, What clever hands you have, my dear.

C C C Camp
Constance

CLEVELAND   NEW YORK
European Representatives Bosworth & Co. London

V.

From an Indian Lodge.

I've tried to abide by the hornet and wren,
but after supper Erastus sneaks me into his
bunk and how willingly I go. He has a mouth
on him and a darling set of dancing legs.
When he first kissed me at the dance he said,
I'm comin' in, like it was a military maneuver
of sorts, but in the bunkhouse he is changed,
all nerves and mentation; he folds my cardigan
like a funeral flag, real serious. He folds
my brassiere in half too, makes a bowl of it,
sticks his glasses in, then pauses in the chill
to look at me. I can hear the ruckus out at
the bonfire, and some of its light bathes the
wooden walls, persimmoning them. They call
those licking flames, he says. Up goes that
sweet-talking mouth on my belly and I forget all about Poland. Down go his hands and
my clever ones too. I have tried to be good
but I let him lead, just like when we jitterbug, and we laugh a little, like when we
jitterbug, and get carefree and dewy like
how we do and he almost knocks me unconscious
by lifting me up and setting me down
someplace else, accidentally banging my head
on a post that still has bark on it. He says,
Aw Jeez, sorry doll, but we don't stop to
check for blood, we keep   saltating.

Erastus Lon

PITHOLE CORDUROYED ITS STREETS ON ACCOU

I love how you care about animals

THE HORSES LOST THEIR HAIR AND DIED BECAUSE THE TE
THERE WERE BROTHELS LINING A WHOLE BLOCK HE

Could we be kissing where a

Let me warm your hands.   THE WIND

cheeks are aflame.

TOWN AND TOOK THEIR HOU

Someday we'll get

JOHN WILKES BOOTH OW
BEFORE HE BREEZED

EVENTUALLY PITHOL

We'll buy a

THEY TOOK THE MET

God is paying

Constance FE

THIS WAS THE ERIE
BOOM BUT THEY WE
BEAVER WARS

Nº1 LUCIA DI LA
2 ROBERT LE
3 NORMA
4 BELISARIO
5 A SONNA

THEY WERE AT AN
HAD NO GUNS
POISON TIPPED.

BUT NO GUNS, AND THE
FACE OF GODS G

me

8
10

Honey whats

CONSTANCE, MY DARL
DRAFT, I'VE JOIN

Constance

ike your corduroys

TERRIBLE MUD BUT CORDUROYING WAS A DANGER TO THE HORSES

stalking while I

NEGLECTED THEM *You know everything*

THE BOOM

once stood? THEY BUILT A HOTEL IN A SINGLE DAY

D OF A FIRE AND BURNED UP THE TOWN *My*

HO STILL HAD SHELTER ABANDONED THE

THEM IF THEY COULD

se, with?

OF A WELL IN PITHOLE

A PRESIDENT.

FOR $4.37

then!

URCH DOWN *So*

heed at all, let's

LAND BEFORE THE

HTERED IN THE

er Wars!

DISADVANTAGE. THEY

s? POSSIBLY

Cupid's

WIPED OFF THE

ARTH

ing you?

RL, I'VE HAD THE

MBARDI   JERUSALEM
A FILLE DU REGIMENT
I PURITANI
LA PROPHETE
NABUCODONOSOR
DON GIOVANNI
LA MUETTE DI PORTICI   MASSANNIELO
ZAUBERFLOTE   MAGIC FLUTE
HAYDEE   THE SECRET
20 CHARLES VI

E.

CHYPRE

ERASTUS

50 cnet

JLD
164 Chesnut St

D.A TRUAX
Cincinnati

you

dearest connie darling girl, i
just received your letter and the
lock of hair. i will carry the curl
everywhere, cutting off a lock was
not a bit foolish, for it means
        the world to me. i am glad
        to hear you are staying in
    nights but it must be hard on y
    you dear. connie it takes your
letters an eternity to reach me
here. connie when i asked you to
wait im did mean it, of course i
know what it means to ask a girl
to marry and i do hope to marry you
someday if you will have me. i
am in no condishion to ask you
now, for we-- as you said-- are
to young. you know as well as i
that when i go across i might
not come back. but you can bet i
will do everything in my power
to come back. you are the closest
thing in the world to me, i wear
you like my skin. i love my
parents but my love for you is
much different connie. i hope
i am not making a mistake by
    telling you this but i said i
would never lie so i may as well
tell you the way i

would like things to be.
i know connie it is serious and
i did not think i would talk
about it for quite some time
but you must know how great my
love is for you now. i would
marry you tomorrow if you would s
    say the word. i have to see
you once more before i leavel---
    i have to. i'm afraid to talk
like this but it's all true.
please write and say you will
            wait.
        yes or no.
s   darling girl i pray i
will be yes.   i have to go into
town for the pictures. they were
ready last night but i'm having
yours colored. i've poured my
heart out here and i hope i did
not make a mistake. if your
family sees this letter they will
never let me see you again
and i never want that to happen
in a million   years,
so you'd best bury it   under
Our Tree. i will
close for tonight   DEAR
and you will
hear from me three-
tomorrow and the day after
that, as long as i have paper
and pen and hands to hold them
with, my wild rose, my constance.

        love,
                    EB

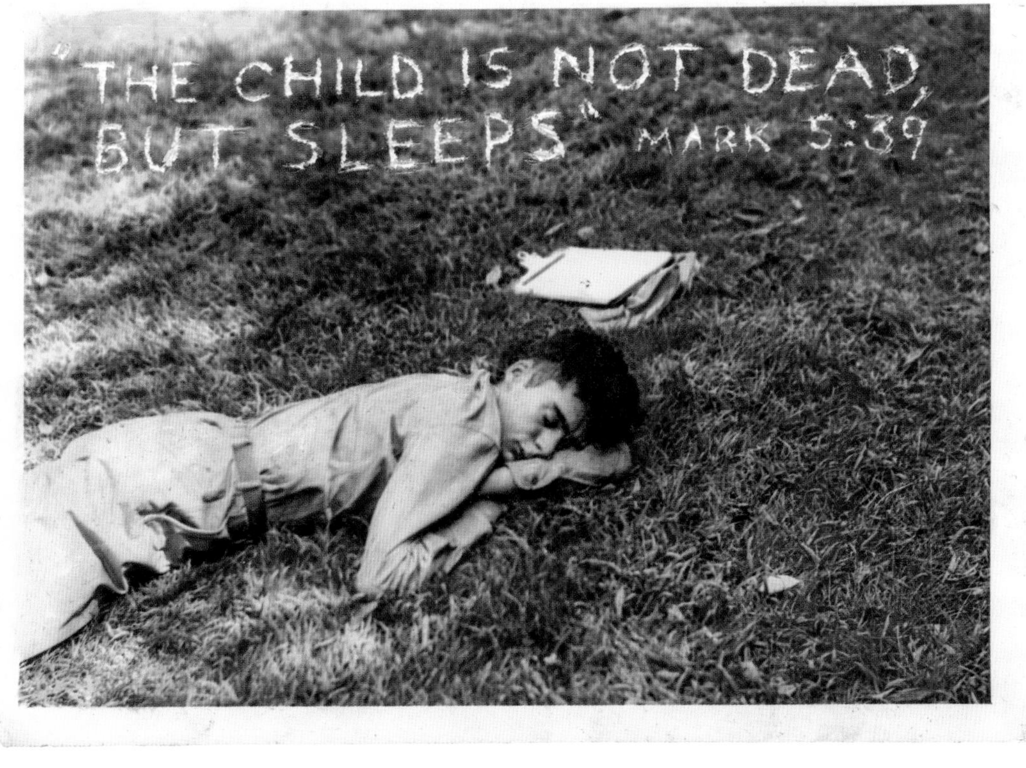
"THE CHILD IS NOT DEAD,
BUT SLEEPS" MARK 5:39

A-pella 2, 3, 4; Interclass Basket
Spring Concerts 2, 3, 4; Amateur Broadcast (vocal) 1, 2
Committee 3; Mystery Pla
oes 3. Guidan

There's a deep, si-lent riv-er
O'er its dark, foaming wa-ters

Mouse is walking her across the bridge.
His shirt is tucked in nicely. Her
saddleshoes are not the best for walking, but not the worst. The small of her
back is how he must guide her home, but
What is the small, he wonders. She swats
his hand away. He lied about fixing a
ridehome in the quarterback's packard,
that much he tells her. Her cardigan is
unbuttoned, color of mashed peas, she
folds her arms into it now, restraining
herself. Her profile, which was so gay
in the auditorium, is petulant. How do
you breath out of a nose that small, he
teases. Little piglet. A sliver of moon.
She's limping a bit from the blisters.
Her daddy will be livid. Mouse thinks
the sore feet are from all that dancing,
which is not what she claims. The holes
in her face are watering, she stops
abruptly and turns away, looking over
the rail into the blackening river.
She's acting very spoiled. He comes up
behind her, only to comfort her, only
to comfort her,

comes up behind her to comfort, he
comes up behind her, only to comfort,

PETROLEUM BRIDGE

HE COMES UP BEHIND HER, "ONLY TO COMFORT"
ONLY TO COMFORT ONLY TO COMFORT ONLY TO COMFORT
ONLY TO COMFORT HE TOLD THE OFFICERS "ONLY
TO COMFORT" ONLY TO COMFORT HER

PROM QUEEN'S TRAGIC
FALL FROM PETROLEUM
BRIDGE RULED ACCIDENT
BY TOWNSHIP POLICE

PITTSBURGH, PA.   23 Oct.
‎_____   _____
        (Induction station)   (Date)

                    This is to advise you that
BROTHER MOUSE   43036765   has been
‎_____   _____
             (Name)   (Army Serial No. if accepted)

*~~selected for active military service and returned to his home.~~
* accepted for active military service.   He has left this station en route to a reception

center at _____RC. FT. GEORGE G. MEADE, MD._____ where he will
remain for a short time and then be sent to another station.   As he will be in transit for
the next few days, it will be difficult for mail to reach him.   It is therefore requested
that no attempt be made to communicate with him except in an emergency until
you receive further advice as to the address to which mail for him should be sent.

‎_____

    This card to be made out and mailed at induction station at time of transfer
therefrom.   "Off I go to kill the Krauts", said he,
* Strike out clause not applicable.   goose-stepping at the station.

W. D., A. G. O. Form No. 202
        August 7, 1942   ★ 16—18394-2   U. S GOVERNMENT PRINTING OFFICE

Biggerstaff, Erastus b. Pithole, PA
You see— d. 1942

He was killed—in the War.
In the summer of 1939, Erastus worked for the
Civilian Conservation Corps in Sligo, PA. He
was known by his friends as "Boomba". During
high school he could be found at the
dance halls where he was well-known
for his dancing skills, particularly the
jitterbug.

They wouldn't let me marry him because I was
seventeen when he went away. I thought I
was a widow in some way.

Killed in action in Italy, near Pianaro.

I was never his in any way at all.

CONNIE
Chemistry Club, 4; Ama-
teur Broadcast, 3, 4;
Home Room Secretary, 3;
Student Council, 2; Drum
Majorette, 2, 3, 4; A
Cappella, 2, 3, 4; "Tune
In" "Faust"; "Carmen";
Concerts, 2, 3, 4; String
Quartet, 3, 4; North-
western Violin Solo, 2, 3,
4; Secretary Senior Nomi-
nating Committee; Junior
Prom Committee; Christ-
mas Card Committee, 4;
Girls' Bowling League, 4;
Orchestra, 2, 3, 4; Sec-
retary, 4.
Connie, with the big brown
eyes and beautiful smile,
is a song bird as well as
an accomplished violinist.
Her sunny disposition has
won her many friends.

Most of the boys in town got their
cards and are coming home on last
leaves or the way poor Erastus did, as a
ghost. There's no one left to dance
with save ⅍ 4Fs and codgers.
His mother had a little vial
to save her tears in. I was a
dumb cow at the service, looking about with dry eyes and
nothing but scorched air in
my throat. It wasn't much of
a turnout. I told a lie to get
there, and then had nothing
useful to say. Was it wrong to
put a feather in my hat? Erastus
found it on one of our forest
walks, such a fancy blue in it,
like stormy skies, like nobody's
eyes. His were brown and glowed
like Seraphino's purfling, his
were consuming as quicksand. And
~~now the whole of him underground~~ ~~underwater~~
~~a thought I cant~~
He said it was nothing special, a common
feather from a common jay. When I got
home, Mama tore the hat off my head and
took some hair with it.

*May your life be ever blue and
~~warm~~ Sun, making all natural
on Studling cheerfulness meet
wound. And may reflect slow
from that be a source of nature
to you in creation through
true. Adieu*

Our father, papa of us all to the best
of our knowledge,
    great pale immigrant
hands   knobbled closed from working the rails

Didn't he drag us through the dirty thirties
and because of his hardships, didnt we try harder
                            to fathom him

                    his grabbing &
        his   smacking

He had in one PALM proof of the Pennsylvania
rails and mines; embedded in his violet-pink
skin was a tiny lump of coal, India ink black,

the size of a tick. Do you remember it?

Thinking of that diabolical speck from the

olden-olden changes my coloring.

Pa had the gout and the pressured blood
and that sly
story   at the ready in his palm.
    "See how hard those bastards worked me,"", he would say
and into his bowled hands a girl might blink,
as into a fairy pond, bewitched.

Passenger Train Supplies

25   Tons Hard Coal   4 50   112 50

--o, sister--

you are asleep
with your mouth agape
but your fingers scale
the agony box   doe ray me

in our icy room
i am listening
for something else
a thing not musical
is it coming?

i'd rather never
read his palm
but if i close my eyes
he mashes my face and his hands
smell of limburger
my senses are despoiled
for the rest of my days
i will not breathe deep
or speak easy -
from my pillow i learn
the way the goose died
calamus, dewlap, pennae
grassy droppings and gunpowder
chivvying my nose
and now to my ears
come hard soles
down the hall
o, sister

Do you like secrets? Most girls do, s‹
I think you must like them. I also th
‹‹u can keep them; at any rate, ‹

***
* MJG *
***

"girls have secrets,
men have honor"

Shout! Wherever You May Be
I AM AN AMERICAN

Words and Music by
IRA SCHUSTER
PAUL CUNNINGHAM
LEONARD WHITCUP

Marcia moderato

STAGE NAME: Connie Gale

EXPLAIN HOW YOU GOT YOUR START IN
SHOW BUSINESS AND THE HIGH SPOTS OF
YOUR CAREER:

Mama dressed us up and found work for
us when we were just out of diapers so
I can't remember NOT being in show busin

I was born in a theatrical trunk

My mother was stagestruck and

At about four years of age, I saw an

My father would've been a wonderful actor
if he hadn't gone into the drink railroad
mines ministry, and my mother has a lovely singing voice, so I think it came about
naturally. My sister and I have been
performing professionally for many years
now.

WHAT IS THE NATURE OF YOUR ACT?:

I'd play the accordian while riding a
unicycle and balancing a whirlygig
between my teeth to escape this sulphrous
little

Primarily I am a singer and classically
trained violinist.

ACTRESSES***PLEASE DESCRIBE THE COSTUMES
IN YOUR ACT:

From their iron rings Mama pulled down
the draperies

Shout!

AM   AN   A

SKILLFUL MANEUVERING
1. FIND YOURSELF IN THE RIGHT
"GEOGRAPHICAL SPOTS"
2. BE WITH THE GANG *
TWOSOMES ARE NOT THE VOGUE
3. BE WHERE THINGS ARE GOING ON
OUT OF BOUNDS
1. DARK LONESOME CORNERS
2. UPSTAIRS WHEN THE PARTY IS DOWNSTAIRS
3. OUTSIDE INSTEAD OF INSIDE
4. SURROUNDED BY JUST MEN
5. NO DRINKING
6. NO DANCING WHILE WEARING HATS OR WRAPS
7. NO SMOKING ON THE DANCE FLOOR
HOW ABOUT DATING?
(ONE OF YOUR BIGGEST PROBLEMS!)
Would you date this boy if he wore "civies"?
Would you want him coming regularly to your
home? Are you the same kind of people? Is
he satisfied to be with you at the Center
until you know each other better? Is he
anxious to make it clear whether or not he
is married, divorced, or "still in circula-
tion"? (Are you playing fair on this score?)
Can you discriminate? You know you can't
date the whole army, navy and merchant
marine--you can't give a chip off your heart
often and at random and have anything left
for your "big" moment! Can you "take it"
for the duration? You can if you ration
your feelings! You must learn to give
service without giving too much of YOU.
The war may last a long time-it's our job
to make a strong finish-to be on hand when
they come back. It's a big order, but who
wants an easy war job?

also:
1. no dancing with
girls if men are
present
2. no saying no
to a dance
3. buy bobby pins

THE YOUNG MEN'S CHRISTIAN ASSOCIATIONS • THE NATIONAL CATHOLIC COMMUNITY SERVICE
THE SALVATION ARMY • THE YOUNG WOMEN'S CHRISTIAN ASSOCIATIONS
THE JEWISH WELFARE BOARD • THE NATIONAL TRAVELLERS AID ASSOCIATION

USO
UNITED SERVICE ORGANIZATIONS

Sis,
Don't be angry, I'll come back. I'm sorry
to leave you with the Horrible Rodent.
I know Mama's theory is I've gone wild, but
maybe I was born so. Remember what a daredevil I
was on my bicycle? And now you teased me for
yelling, "Look at the feeling!" as I pedaled by,
waving both hands. You can't LOOK at feelings, you
insisted, but I still think otherwise. Maybe as you
read this you will smell summer on Diamond Alley &
taste the fallen jujubes. Remember when my hips
came in too fast and gave me stripes and Pa said
I was a quagga but would be pretty enough for
somebody in the dark? You said, Yet another reason
to keep yer bloomers on. Or how bout when Mr. G was
photographing and I pretended to have a bad dream
under the willow so's you could rest, and as he

laughed we saw his wayback teeth (which looked like
rubbish bins) and you said, The closer one gets
to a Frenchman, the less romantic it is? Remember
when you hid his crutch? And when we got into the
ice cream at the church pageant? Such a wicked little
fairy.
        I will salt away our memories, even the
jaggedly ones I'll turn over and over until they
are burnished. They are jewels to me dear.
We are the bridge in a song, sis, forever linked,
together we make music and there is nothing and
no one can asunder us, not even war! Plus now
you'll have all the blankets to yourself.

                    Love, Connie

INSTRUCTIONS

CHECK ONE OF EACH OF THE SQUARES AS DESIRED
OR FILL IN BLANK SPACES.   PLACE DATE HERE

☐ DEAR GEORGE/TOM/DICK/HARRY
☐ FREIND " "   YOUR NAME
☐ SOLDIER   Connie

RECIEVED YOUR ☐→NICE LETTER ☐→DOPEY LATTER
TODAY. ☐→I WAS PLEASED TO HERE FROM YOU ☐→I
WASNT PLEASED AT ALL ☐→I HOPE YOUR FEELING
FINE ☐→I HOPE YOU HAVE THE MISERIES ☐→I AM STILL
SINGLE ☐→I AM ENGAGED. ☐→I AM MARRIED. I WOULD
☐→LIKE ☐→NOT LIKE TO HEAR FROM YOU AGAIN
THE WEATHER LATELY HAS BEEN ☐→NICE ☐→FAIR
☐→BAD MY MOM + DAD SAY ☐→HELLO ☐→GO TO—!
MY BROTHER IS ☐→STILL IN ☐→DISCHARGED. I
☐→FINISHED ☐→AM STILL GOING TO SCHOOL. I'M
☐→NOT WORKING ☐→WORKING AT _____.
I ☐→RECIEVED ☐→DID NOT RECIEVE YOUR ☐→NICE
☐→UNCOMPLEMENTARY VALENTINE. ☐→THANKS ALOT
☐→NO THANKS AT ALL. I AM ☐→SORRY ☐→GLAD
☐→UNCONCERNED THAT I DIDNT GET A CHANCE
TO TALK TO YOU WHILE YOU WERE HOME ON FURLO.
SO LONG + ☐→WRITE AGAIN ☐→WRITE IF YOU LIKE
(IT WONT DO YOU ANY GOOD) ☐→DONT WRITE (IT DEF-
INATELY WONT BE ANSWERED.
PLEASE   NOTE: THE FOLLOWING SPACE ON
THIS SIDE + OTHER SIDE RESERVED FOR
ADDITIONAL COMMENT. IF ANY, I HOPE

Dear Connie,

This morning two hundred more women marines came here. They have a swell uniform but I do not like the idea of women being in the service. Of course they are doing a good job but I would rather see them home. I hate it down here and so does everyone else from the North so I don't see how a woman can stand it. But maybe a woman can stand more than I think.

Love,

Dear Connie,

You said in your letter that you'd like a snapshot of me "if l'd send it". You know darn well I'd send you the city of Denver if you asked me. I'm still the same jerk who used to bother you when I was a civilian. Oh how I wish I was a dirty civilian once more. Do you remember the night we were sitting on the running board of a car on Bissell Ave and Janice was up the street necking with Loving Thomas (the dear boy) and you told me you were a good girl with bigger plans, well now I see how serious you were. You've probably forgotten all of this but I havent. My barracks is right in back of the landing field and there's a plane burning over there which means I'd better go. Love,

Bill

We are in a real swamp
and it is infested with
rattlesnakes and copper-
heads. This morning we
killed a nest of young
rattlers. I have to buy a
hunting knife. We were
told to buy a good one
because someday in the
near future we are going
to use them.
A letter from a fellow's
girl can sure buck him
up, by the by.

Love,
Clyde

The other day we came
back here to tent city
and it sure is cold.
There were 300 of us and
yesterday they took all
but 30 of us. So they
took the best friend of mine.
You remember Stanley, well,
they took him.
we are not allowed
to write where they
went or anything
about it.
love,

DAVE

For the last couple of days
my so-called morale has
been right down at the
bottom. Afterall, when
you get NO at mail call
for 5 days in a row, it
gets pretty discouraging.
I was lying in bed thinking
of you and the boys started
a crap game at the foot
of my bed so I couldnt
sleep. That's why I'm
writing you at 2:30 in the
morning. I'm a tired son
of a gun right now
but how am I supposed
to sleep with a pair
of dice rattling in my
ear? If I had any $$$$$$$
I would be in that
game, but I'm broke. If
you ever feel disgusted
& need a good laugh
just look at the
enclosed picture.

                    Lee-
                    love,
                    ED

The main reason I'm
writing this letter is
to tell you that
you're not going to hear
from me for a long time,
it won't be because I don't
want to write you, you know
better than that, and hope-
fully it won't be because
I'm pushing up daisies on
some island in the Pacific.
Heck Connie, I don't even
know if they grow daisies
there. You said in your
letter there are only
2 year old boys, Four F's
and codgers left in town,
but youre not in PA anymore
so I imagine you are swim-
ming in boyss in NY and
elsewhere. I hope you are
having a swell time
        on the road and
not getting in too thick
with the GIs.
                    Love,
                    Freddie

Darling,

Every right you can hear
some fellow crying like a
child in his hammock. I'm
not crying but it was in
fact one week ago I had the
boxing match on base and it
did not do my shoulder any
good. I am happy to report
the other fellow was bleeding so bad they had to stop
the fight so I was declared
Winner. Today on the obstacle
course I got a nice black eye.
This is a terrible place and
the eats are rotten. How's
the weather Darling? That
word Darling sure is coming
 in handy and it ~~feels~~ makes
me feel good to use it.

Love,
George

Dear, You are r ight for I am in the
hospital again and have been here for
 some time now. The last time I wrote
 you i was here then too but did not
want to say nothing to nobody. i was here
a few week s before i even told my family
 as soon as i get out of the hospital i
will make Corporal. did your brother get
promoted yet? i got a frame for your picture andit is on my bed table next to me
how is ▭? ▭? gee i sound nosy.
Connie I may as well tell you the truth
for i am not doing so well. the doc seem
to ~~think~~ doubt t ere is any cure so jus
 what will happen i am not sure. Please
    excuse   the blots for i am all mixed
up. and I am sure now i will have to get
another operation before i can even thin
of going back to duty. I hear from ▭
you might go overseas. I should be going
not you, it s not right. Honey I must
confess that night by the lake I made
 you think we ran out of gas by pullin
pulling the choke. honey quite a bit of
work has been done on my head and that
is my only excuse for my handwriting. I
think i would feel much better if they
 would leave me alone and stop opening
my head up like a ~~pumpkin~~ jackolantern
  but I know it s all for my own good
d so I will do whatever they want. From
 my point of view everything is perfect
 between us and sorry e if you think
  I took your last letter wrong by
 calling it a DEAR JOHN.

LOVE,
Hank

Dear Connie,
Remember after I saw your show I told
you I was starting to enjoy this war
because you are in it? Well, I still
stand by that sentiment but alot
has transpired since then.
On our way back from the Panama Canal
we saw a little action: A German sub
attacked our convoy late one night/ it
fired two tin fish at one of the merchant ships but missed/ then the fun
started/ our ship and two sub chasers
went out after the sub/ we sent out
flares and the sub chasers dropped
ash cans./ the kraut sub came to the
surface and we opened fire/ they ~~xxxx~~
opened up with their deck gun /one of
the ash cans   musta caused
damage otherwise it wouldnt have come
up again./   they only
fired a few   shots then
went under   again /their
fire came close   to the other
ship but not   so near us/
I shot a few   rounds at
the sub myself,   but I was
too excited to   be much good
and it was nearly   out of range
—Well, the   chasers
stayed in the area of where the sub
was last seen dropping cans, but we
dont know yet if we got the sub or
not.
We docked in Los Angeles for one nigh
long enough for one liberty and of
course we hit Hollywood, I had a
swell time at the Hollywood Canteen,
there were so many movie stars floating around we just stood there
speechless but none were as good-
looking as you Connie Gale, cross
my heart.

Love, Iz

TO A SOLDIER WHO'S TOO BUSY TO WRITE

Dear ☐,
Here I am in the dear old Midwest. Our unit
was broken up. Our last show was in South
Bend, Indiana. I could join another unit in
this country but have decided to go "Over
the Puddle." I'm to report in New York on
the 25th. There's so much to be done before
I go. We've no idea where we'll go, of
course, whether it will be Europe or the
Pacific. I've already passed my physical
and had my passport photos taken. Speaking
of pictures, ☐ has been unable to get
film for her camera. If I have time in New
York, I'd love to have some nice ones
made. I'll be so very busy though.
How do you like ☐ by now? I hope that
your ☐ is getting better and better.
How on earth did you happen to hurt it
again? You asked me to excuse your writing
boners. Murder, I'm the world's worst, I
do believe. ☐ and I are trying to
get on the same unit, but I don't know if
we'll be successful or not. It will help
to have someone I know along. We're keeping
our fingers crossed. We had a good time in
☐. I hope the fellows at ☐ are
as nice as those at ☐.

Fold Here   Fold Here

DEAR_____

I AM FEELING_____
GOOD, BAD, INDIFFERENT

Signed *Constance*

P. S.   Do write soon. Perhaps
         the next letter I receive
         will be in France, or
         Italy, or somewhere.

              Love,

Miss Constance Gale
Camp Shows Inc.
JJ #54 8 West 40th St.
N.Y., 18, N.Y.

IDLE GOSSIP SINKS SHIPS

SO FOR NOW ILL CLOSE

☐→ LOVE (AM I KIDDING)

☐→ AS EVER

☐→ SINCERELY

☐→ KINDEST REGARDS

Constance ← SIGN HERE

the town

some buildings still standing

remains of bridge leading to nowhere

water

the poor Italians

cables and rubble

Connie G.

Ponte Santa Trinita, Florence
Italy

P.S. Allies are putting a "portable"
bridge atop to cross the Arno
("Holy Trinity" Bridge)

Wish you
were here!

Tonight about midnight, we commence the attack on Sicily, and we will go to General Quarters in every sense of the word. Full battle condition Afirm will be set.

In general, we may expect the following:
1. Enemy mines.
2. "E" boats and submarines.
3. There may be shelling from the beach.
4. There may be aircraft attacks (especially at dawn).
5. There may possibly be attacks by other surface craft.

NIELDS mission is to screen   thern attack by the enemy.

All hands take particular in   al care. The instructions
that have been given you are   d that is for your health
and safety. Have gas masks,   tment, flame-proof
clothing, life jackets etc.   hat covers all possible
parts of your skin to preven   rself and your station.
Have everything in 100% work   ones, your gear and
station today. Test everyth

CAUTION! During darkness, we may be fired upon. We must avoid giving our
position away if it dama.   uccess. During darkness the following orders
    5" - 38 will be fire
    40-MM - Same.
    20-MM - Same. (not
    Torpedoes fired whe
    Depth charges fi
    Smoke screens laid

INDEX.   287

Life, uncertain. 260, 262, 324.
    christian. 251 to 259, 329.
Lord's Day, (see Sabbath)
    supper 199, 393 to 399.
Love, divine. 152, 10 to 122.

Repentance. 266, 267, 413, 414.
Resignation. 124, 125, 153, 179, 266, 281, 431 to 433.
Resolution. 419, 420.
Retirement, religious. 150, 385, 265.
Religion. 226.

Sabbath. 9, 10, 16, 21, 22, 32.
Safety in God. 390

During daylight:
    The above will be f   ee, a definite
    target - and this o   nger our own forces.
    We must get the Arm   ments by embarassing
    shooting.

Never fire on aircraft th   ll have hundreds of
our own planes above us.   ose that have not
dropped their bombs yet,   ngerous.

The assault will be toni   r from 3 to 6 days
while transports are unlo   during that time.
After the above period, w   owed by more convoy
duty - but destination s

SUMMARY. Our safety and   's hands - calm -
quiet and deliberate atte   with every energy
you possess. You are fully trained and prepared for battle. Do your job well.
Get all the rest you can, as we will be at General Quarters all night and
perhaps for days.

Knowing and carrying out the above will insure us of positive and quick success.

Good luck and good shooting to all hands.

 , Italy

Dear Sis,
            Whatever you do, don't
let Mama get ahold of this, Top Secret!

I must've been out of my mind bringing
the white crepe here. Italy is muddier
than Pithole, PA. It's true we are stay-
ing (for now) in a palace but it's got
no heat and all around us is blown to
bits. There are empty pedestals in the
square, some of them with just the marble
toes of a God remaining. Yesterday on our
way to ████████ we passed a group of
women cutting up a dead German horse with
kitchen knives. All of them had on blue
aprons covered in mud and blood. The head
of the animal was tossed to the side,
though I suspect it will be used for soup.
In spite of this, I'm afraid I've contract-
ed the "social disease" they warned us
about in training. The fellows are so
nice. Besides the USO shows, our duties
include dancing with them, listening to
their miseries, and keeping them away
from the local ██████ most of whom were
perfectly nice girls before this started and are only bad now because they are
starving to death. It's hard not to fall
for the GIs, unless you are Toni, who
has quite the knack with a pencil and
spends hours sketching in her bunk. She
got called into active duty when we played the hospital in ██████ and the portrait
artist didnt show. Sometimes those drawings
are the last a mother sees of her son.
Imagine. (Speaking of, I heard our brother
got sent home. What'd he do?!) I'm
still sketching bridges but they are
mostly bombed out.

                                    ⟶

Toni and Betty spend a lot of
time trying to stay "natural"
blonds for the duration, so for
once I'm thrilled to have witch's
hair, as Mama calls it. It's hard
to come by beauty supples on the
black market. We tear up if we
drop a hairpin in the mud, they
cost so much to replace. I've
already run out of hair flowers
as we're encouraged to throw them
to the boys for keepsakes. They
go wild. Irene thinks we can get
more in ████, or at least the
fabric to make them with. I've
so much to tell you and so little
time here. Please excuse the
wobbles, I'm in a Jeep. How is the
Big Apple? If you are not too busy,
you can write me c/o the Camp Shows
address on 40th, #52, Blues Busters
Unit.

Love,

Constance

PASTIFICIO CURCURUTO & F⁰ IL RIVENDITORE HA L'OBBLIGO DI PESARE IL PAC-

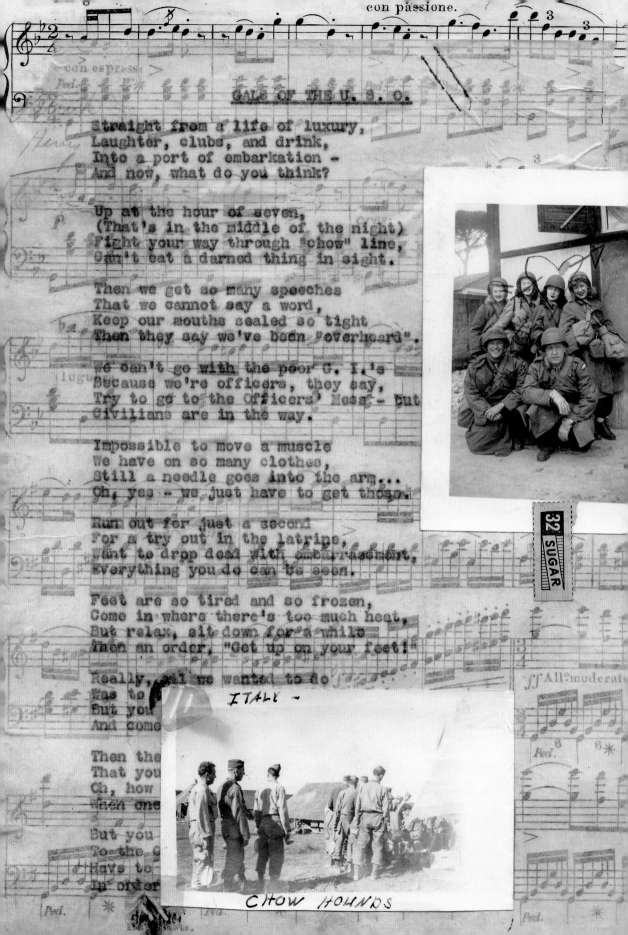

GALS OF THE U. S. O.

Straight from a life of luxury,
Laughter, clubs, and drink,
Into a port of embarkation -
And now, what do you think?

Up at the hour of seven,
(That's in the middle of the night)
Fight your way through "chow" line,
Can't eat a darned thing in sight.

Then we get so many speeches
That we cannot say a word,
Keep our mouths sealed so tight
Then they say we've been "overheard".

We can't go with the poor G. I.'s
Because we're officers, they say,
Try to go to the Officers' Mess - but
Civilians are in the way.

Impossible to move a muscle
We have on so many clothes,
Still a needle goes into the arm...
Oh, yes - we just have to get those.

Run out for just a second
For a try out in the latrine,
Want to drop dead with embarrassment,
Everything you do can be seen.

Feet are so tired and so frozen,
Come in where there's too much heat,
But relax, sit down for a while
Then an order, "Get up on your feet!"

Really, all we wanted to do
Was to
But you
And come

Then the
That you
Oh, how
When one

But you
To the
Have to
In order

Get back to the barracks at midnight
To rest your tired bones and then
Before you get a chance to close an eye
You're up starting it over again.

Oh, what the heck, we don't care,
We'll keep going till we fall,
'Cause it's for those marvellous guys,
And we love nothing more, after all!

... by Toni

7, 19

drawn by Toni for me when we were in Florence

He struts around shirtless
as much as he can, showing off
his new muscles. No, that's
not true at all. The other boys
tower over him, just like they
did at Oil City High. His back
aches from standing up straight &
he'd sleep in his uniform if he
had his druthers.

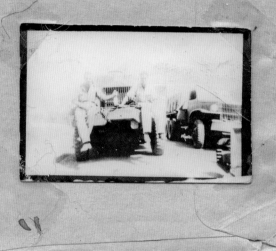

Our brother's
druthers are a
dangerous thing

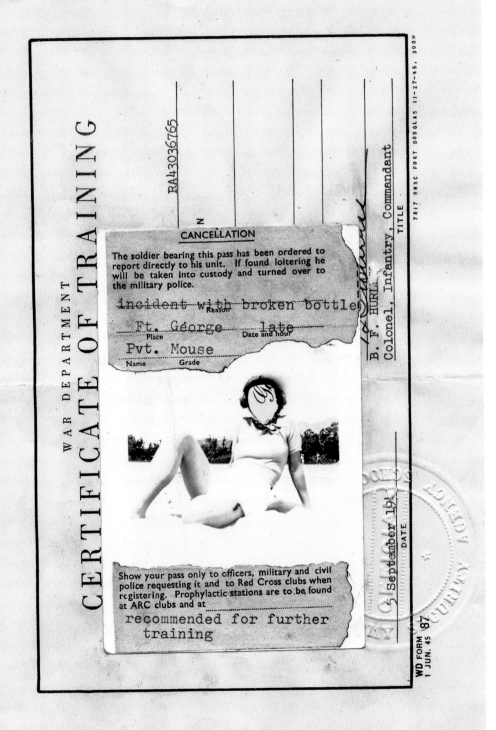

WAR DEPARTMENT

CERTIFICATE OF TRAINING

RA4303676S

7817 HHSC FORT DOUGLAS 11-27-45, 300M

B. F. HURL

Colonel, Infantry, Commandant

TITLE

CANCELLATION

The soldier bearing this pass has been ordered to report directly to his unit. If found loitering he will be taken into custody and turned over to the military police.

~~incident with broken bottle~~
Reason

Ft. George   late
Place   Date and hour

Pvt. Mouse
Name   Grade

Show your pass only to officers, military and civil police requesting it and to Red Cross clubs when registering. Prophylactic stations are to be found at ARC clubs and at

recommended for further training

5 September 19

DATE

WD FORM 87
1 JUN. 45

Oh Sis,
the bridges, the bridges!
The   planted   under
every bridge save one, The
      br   took three blasts to fall.
                  was filled with
      crying dogs and children,
            pots and pans and   . S
ɪɪ complains this is war in a "goddang museum" &
        true   the rubble   a certain beauty
once   are ɪ removed. In   , the
castle's garden still had some frosty vegetables
so we added beans to the rations.
        Last night the Bluesbusters played the Sky
Room in   , what a night
      sin to be happy here.   Our job
jolly under pressure   nurses and the girl
next door,   supposed to be an act
Toni   perfect harmonies   not quite
        you   but almost

      We   I
            with ink made from walnut shells
      cobblestone stained with wine or berries but
      of course there is no fruit in   now. If
indeed it   surely a dog would've
-the ribs of every mammal visible here.
        The more I see of this   , the less I
understand why P   still claims to be German and
as for Mama   thousands of
  crates are filled with rescued artifacts, but what
of the crated   ?? I've had to stop the violin
because a string broke and ther's no getting a
fresh one.
                        Love,
                          C.

Connie, I would write
you just about everyday
if you would answer my
    letters. I have to wash
my clothes tonight and we
also have to wash the floor.
That's where you would
    come in good, you
could wash my clothes,
    make the bed, and
ix all the jobs a girl
should f   do.

                    Love,

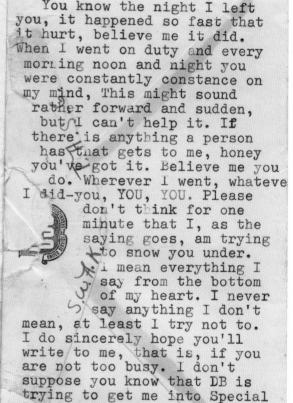

You know the night I left
you, it happened so fast that
it hurt, believe me it did.
When I went on duty and every
morning noon and night you
were constantly constance on
my mind, This might sound
  rather forward and sudden,
    but I can't help it. If
    there is anything a person
    has that gets to me, honey
    you've got it. Believe me you
      do. Wherever I went, whateve
I did-you, YOU, YOU. Please
        don't think for one
        minute that I, as the
        saying goes, am trying
        to snow you under.
        I mean everything I
        say from the bottom
        of my heart. I never
        say anything I don't
mean, at least I try not to.
I do sincerely hope you'll
write to me, that is, if you
are not too busy. I don't
suppose you know that DB is
trying to get me into Special
Services, so he tells me. Are
you working hard? Give my love
to Toni, Irene and Betty and
luck to Jimmy and Wayne.
                    Love,

PS:
What does "As Ever"
mean? I hear d
it's something
awful.

love,

LOUIS

U.S.N   FREE

IT WAS FUN WHEN
I CARRIED YOU AND
YOU WERE
NOT HEAVY
A BIT.

LOVE,

Melvin

Today I am a world away from the
wretched commerce of Naples but it
was just a boatride

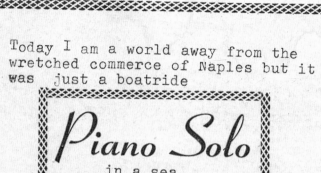

Piano Solo

in a sea

PRICE 40¢

fathoms and fathoms
deep

Little sister, a fathom is the
length of my outstretched arms,
fixin to hug, fixin to jump,
fixin to fly. Such enchantment
here. The blues are nothing like
our Pennsylvania blues. It's
hard to fathom the fathoms, dear,
and the ancient hues, the blues.
Indigo, aquamarine, lapis lazul-
forgive me, I haven't slept.
Black, blacker blue, emerald blue.
We arrived in Capri yesterday
afternoon and were put up at the
La Palma Hotel, where they fed us
cuttlefish-inked spaghetti and
cocktails that tasted foul as
Mama's depression soups. We also
ate sea urchins, still wiggling
when they brought them to the table.
Wayne put one on his head and
wore it like a hat all night.
It suited him- made
his eye- lashes
stand out.

PUBLISHED BY
BELWIN INC,
NEW YORK, U.S.A.

Printed in U.S.A.

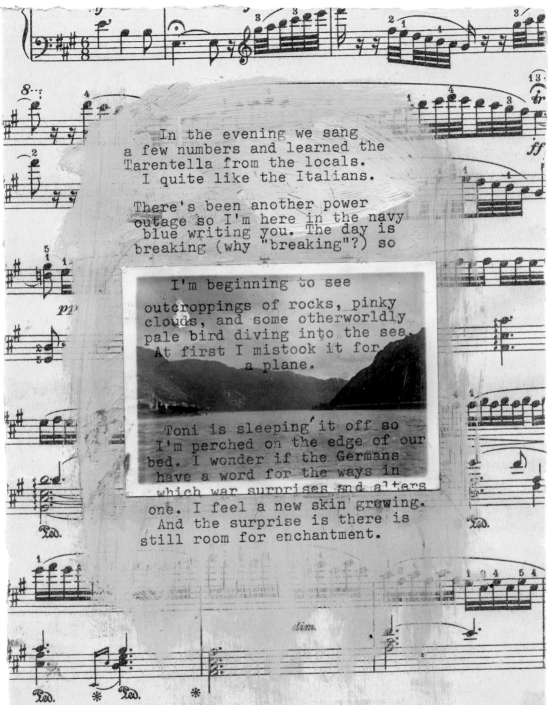

In the evening we sang
a few numbers and learned the
Tarentella from the locals.
I quite like the Italians.

There's been another power
outage so I'm here in the navy
blue writing you. The day is
breaking (why "breaking"?) so

I'm beginning to see

outcroppings of rocks, pinky
clouds, and some otherworldly
pale bird diving into the sea.
At first I mistook it for
a plane.

Toni is sleeping it off so
I'm perched on the edge of our
bed. I wonder if the Germans
have a word for the ways in
which war surprises and alters
one. I feel a new skin growing.
And the surprise is there is
still room for enchantment.

.563-8
Key of A

Sis,

Tonight's <u>MENU</u>:

Roast Partridge

Frog legs and foraged dandelion greens

K Rations

~~Le Pamplemousse au Kirsch~~

Black Market Sparkling Wine

Cheese and Oregano

~~Le Consommé des Viveurs en Tasse~~

Luigi lured and shot about six warblers

~~Le Suprême de Turbot Granville~~

I could not bring myself to try. By
some miracle he also brought some

~~Le Dindonneau Poêlé Avignonnaise~~

"Mozzarella", cheese made from buffalo
milk and molded to resemble the balls

~~Le Céleri Frais à la Flamande~~

of the animal , and "taste like it too"
he said in his charming accent, and

~~La Salade Andalouse~~

"feel like the beast on the tongue."
Unlike Papa's Limburger it was quite

~~La Pêche Glacée Cardinal~~

mild, but there was another odor at
our table comingling with the cheese

~~Les Frivolités~~

and amphibians; turns out Sarge "loathes
Italians" and sprayed himself with

~~La Corbeille de Fruits~~

disinfectant before dinner. Whatever
ill he's harboring hasnt stopped him
from adorning his bunk with religious
pictures he lifts from bombed churches.
Once again, I confused a toad for a
gentleman! I feigned a coughing fit
and turned in early.

P.S: That which sings I shall not eat

ST. P....S
AMERICAN CHURCH

Via Nazionale & Via Napoli

ROME

Wonderful sermon

CHAPLAIN JOSEPH L. BROWN, B. A., B. D. - CHAPLAIN IN CHARGE.
MISS JANICE PLOWMAN - ORGANIST.

Luigi and friends

Prelu...
Hym...   Perronet.
Oper...
Conf...   )
Veni...   Kelway.
Psalm...
Lesso...
Bene...   Thiman.
Cree...
Hym...   Newton.
Serm...
Anth...   Villiams.
Bene...
Hym...   Moultrie.

CHOIR   you are
interested speak to Chaplain Brown ... the service.
We are especially in need of feminine voices. Our
rehearsals are held at 6.30 p.m. on Wednesday.

Hi "Paper Doll",

Do you get much chance
to dance? You know I'd
love to "dance with the
dolly with a hole in her
stocking". You're really
wonderful. Until then,
"I'm Making Believe", and
may God Bless you and ~~keep~~
watch over you. "Keep
'em Smiling and Happy".
"Someday I'll Meet You
                    Again".
"I'll Be Seeing You".

"Dig You Later (a-hubba
hubba hubba)". Love,
                    nick

Cc. APO 782 c/o US Army
PS: "I'd rather have a
paper doll to call my own
than have a fickle-minded
real live girl."
f(I'd trade my kid sister
    for a picture of you.)

WHAT'S THIS I HEAR
ABOUT YOU AND TUBBY
    GRUBER????
    HOW DID I HEAR THAT?
I'VE GOT MY OWN GESTAPO
WATCHING YOU. HOW IS
    BETTY GETTING ALONG?
HOW MANY MEN DOES SHE
HAVE ON THE LINE NOW, OR
DOES SHE STILL GO AROUND
    WITH DICK? I THOUGHT THAT
GUY WOULD BE DEAD BY NOW,
OR IS HE? WELL HERE COMES
    THE MESS SERGEANT GIVING
ME THE STINK EYE. HE'S
THE KIND OF GUY WHO GOES
AROUND STICKING PINS INTO
LITTLE BABIES JUST TO HEAR
THEM CRY. I DONT LIKE THIS
PLACE.

                    LOVE,
        (I REALLY MEAN IT)

Owen

no kidding

(Me at mail Call)

Naturally, his wonts are a soldier's, and his
worries are about keeping his own dear body
safe until an honorable discharge. As he snores,
he's ripening the man he will become after the
war--husband, father, proud owner of something
shiny, like an auto shop or a motorboat.
Briefly I picture him at the helm of the
Connie Marie, but my pigeon supper's not sitting
well, and he hasn't the instinct to reach for me
just because I am here I am here, Me, Me,
Constance Marie,   under the Italian stars.

I wake him with the story of a severed hand
stuck on a fencepost in Caserta, the ring taken
along with its finger.   I am in a nightgown of
fraying apricot silk, which feels nice so he
does hold me awhile.

SARGE

Just thought I'd drop you a few
lines to let you know we're all
fine here and I hope you are the
same. I hope you're not sick Connie,
the reason why I said that is be-
caus~ I haven't heard from you in
about two weeks now and I'm beginning to worry about it. Maybe you
have lost all interest in me, well
hope not Connie, because I haven't
lost interest. I think you're pretty
well. Gee Connie, I better stop
writing like this, you may think
Im getting soft again. Well maybe
I am. We all miss you an awful lot,
Connie, and so do I, very much. Aren
Aren't you ever coming back or do
I have to come over and get you, and
I really mean that too, "Stinker".
Gee, why dont you drop me a few line~
, you know that mailbox looks awful
                    funny, what with the
            petrified cobwebs. What do
                    you say, Miss Gale?
  I hope I don't have to wait too
long. The gang sends their regards.

                    Love,

                    Pete

dearest Connie This is my 1st
letter to you and I really dont
know what to say so I hope youll
-bar- bear with me the simplisity
of this little letter. I didnt
get to high school, just finished
grade 8 and quit to go to work,
then I joined the army and that
was my big mistake. If they
found out how old I was am they
would send me home but now that ive
met you I dont want to go.
just had to write to you for you
    dont know what you did to me
      when I first saw you on stage
and spoke to you in the en
cantinecanteen. I tried calling
you at your hotel but it seems
you were very much asleep, i tried
the whole day but didnt have any
  luck. The last time I called you
had just left so I guess your
unit has moved on and Im trying
to make peace with it, Someday,
somehow I hope to meet you
again so I can tell you everyth ng
Sorry about this I never was much
at writing letter's. Love,

                Quincy

                you

Constance,
What kind of sister doesnt
write back to her own
brother when he happens to be
stationed nearby?
When I didn't hear
from you I took matters into my
own hands and called Wayne
so like it or not I'll see you
and your so-called BLUESBUSTERS
at 2100 hr Saturday, at which time
I will make my own assessment as
to ~~the your~~ state of mind and
report the facts as I see them to
whomever I choose, and if need be
forcibly and physically pull you
out of whatever vile muck you've
                        fallen into.

          I've been promoted
          so would apprec-
            iate it if
            you'd stop
            calling me
                MOUSE

Fold
Here

Fold
Here

RSVP
ANSWER-MAIL

Because we know you're busy—and we
want to save you time — We use this
means of finding out how you are —
(add a P.S. if you've time) — Then
just seal it and post it. Its an important
mail from an important male.

I'm keeping an
eye on you.

Natural Color Card Published by Modern-Ad, Butler, Pa.

Pennsylvania's **FLAMING FOLIAGE** attracts
many tourists at this most colorful time of
the year

Color photo by Richard C. Miller

1478

Today I had to build a
pillbox. In case you do not
know what a pillbox is
I will tell you.
It's a big cement box
for a machine gun.
About five men can get
in it and it is real hot
in there when the
machine gun starts
to fire. It takes
all day to make one.

love,
Roger

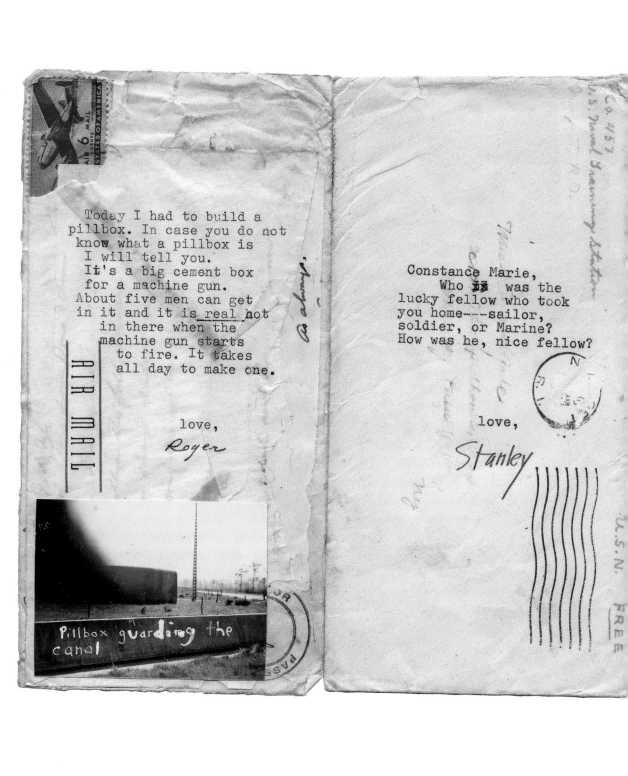

Pillbox guarding the
canal

Constance Marie,
Who ~~is~~ was the
lucky fellow who took
you home---sailor,
soldier, or Marine?
How was he, nice fellow?

love,
Stanley

Beside the bridge, off the track, gone astray:

The English Call it War Aphrodisia, and leave it to the
Brits to make strumpetting sound Shakespearean. If there
is a God, and Sis I grow more skeptical by the hour,
He's a mean one and is tending an Erastus-sized hole in
my chest. Well, He just keeps scooping it out. I've been
sniffing necks to find him again, fibbing into crewcuts,
telling them they smell like pie crust when they smell
like blood   and   mold and hunter and prey.   ,
                              How sweet was my E on the
forest floor, with his merry-go-round tongue. We thought
ourselves such   naughty animals, but we hadn't seen
war. It's not sensical to miss him like this, he was a boy
who couldn't spell condishion.   Yesterday afternoon I saw
                              a mound of children's bones
                              and by nightfall
                                I was singing,
                              but today the thought of
                              his strong, brown hands
                              broke me.

If there wasn't such a thing as music I believe I could forget Erastus,
but halfway across the world they keep
playing our song. Luigi is bringing me
some jam he says will "heal the ferita
from which I still am aching"

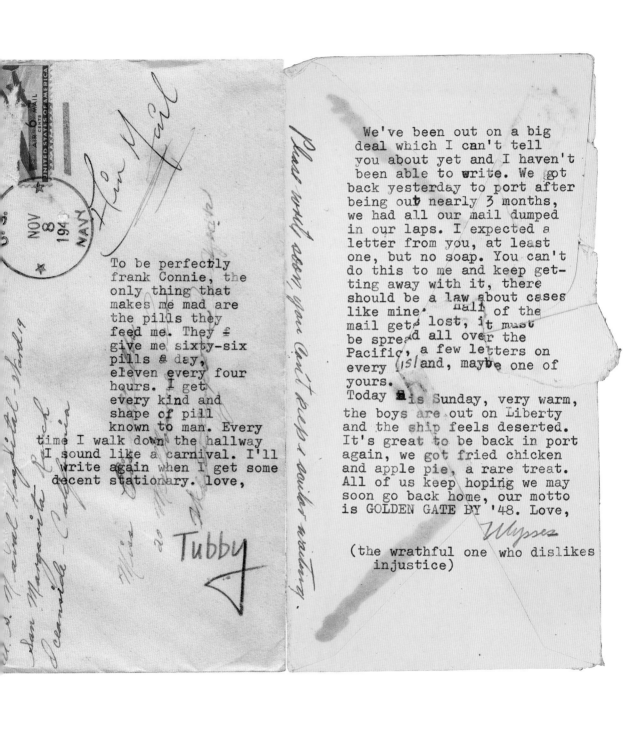

AIR MAIL
6 CENTS
UNITED STATES OF AMERICA

NOV 8 194_
U.S. NAVY

Air Mail

U. S. Naval Hospital Ward 19
San Margarita Rch
Oceanside - California

Please return, you can't resp a worse reading

To be perfectly
frank Connie, the
only thing that
makes me mad are
the pills they
feed me. They £
give me sixty-six
pills a day,
eleven every four
hours. I get
every kind and
shape of pill
known to man. Every
time I walk down the hallway
I sound like a carnival. I'll
write again when I get some
decent stationary. love,

Tubby

We've been out on a big
deal which I can't tell
you about yet and I haven't
been able to write. We got
back yesterday to port after
being out nearly 3 months,
we had all our mail dumped
in our laps. I expected a
letter from you, at least
one, but no soap. You can't
do this to me and keep getting away with it, there
should be a law about cases
like mine. half of the
mail gets lost, it must
be spread all over the
Pacific, a few letters on
every island, maybe one of
yours.
Today is Sunday, very warm,
the boys are out on Liberty
and the ship feels deserted.
It's great to be back in port
again, we got fried chicken
and apple pie, a rare treat.
All of us keep hoping we may
soon go back home, our motto
is GOLDEN GATE BY '48. Love,

Ulysses

(the wrathful one who dislikes
injustice)

ADAGIO

jane doe found
in field

Harvest-mouse. 1/2

Major Areas (See MOS Test Aid DA PAM 1	VERY LOW	LOW	AVER-AGE	HIGH	VERY HIGH
WEAPONS			X		
TACTICS			X		
FIELD ACTIVITIES			X		

AUTHENTICATION
VA DATA
SERVICE
26. DECORATIONS, MEDALS, BADGES, COMMENDATIONS, CITATIONS AND CAMPAIGN RIBBONS AWARDED OR AUTHORIZED
Marksman (Carbine)/National Defense Service Medal/Good Conduct Medal
27. WOUNDS RECEIVED AS A RESULT OF ACTION WITH ENEMY FORCES (Place and date, if known)
None
NA
NA
32. REMARKS
Blood Gr
Item 3a
SSAN: 1
16 W Sou
35a. TYPED NAME, GRADE AND TITLE OF AUTHORIZING OFFICER
D A TAEBEL 2d Lt AGC
b. SIGNATURE OF OFFICER AUTHORIZED TO SIGN
DD FORM 1 NOV 55 214
REPLACES EDITION OF 1 JUL 52, WHICH IS OBSOLETE.
ARMED FORCES OF THE UNITED STATES
REPORT OF TRANSFER OR DISCHARGE
1
IMMEDIATE REENLISTMENT
RE-1
PRIOR SERVICE
49.
BRANCH & CLASS/ ARMED FORCE & COMPONENT
SERVICE NUMBER
DATE ENL, IND, APT, AND/OR OAD
DATE OF DISCHARGE OR RELEASE
GRADE/ RATE OR RANK
TYPE OF DISCHARGE
REASON FOR DISCHARGE
TIME LOST (No. Days)
bottle for a gun. traded his
flyswatter for a bottle, traded his bottle for
traded his flyswatter for a bottle, traded his
DT 144

March 22,
Cures for "Menstrual Blockage"

Cocktails

gin and ginger
Martini Sweet and Dry
turpentine & quinine

San Giorgio
angelica root, unripe papaya

Side Car
drops of pennyroyal

" 173 "

lye
D'Amour

carbolic soap & water
North Nova
epsom salts

Collins, Sours, Fizzes

simmering mustard
Scotch, Rye and Bourbon Whiskies

pickle fork, butter knife, biro
Italian and French Brandies
knitting needle, crochet hook, pen

Choice of Italian and Imported Liquors

scissors broomstick toothbrush prayer

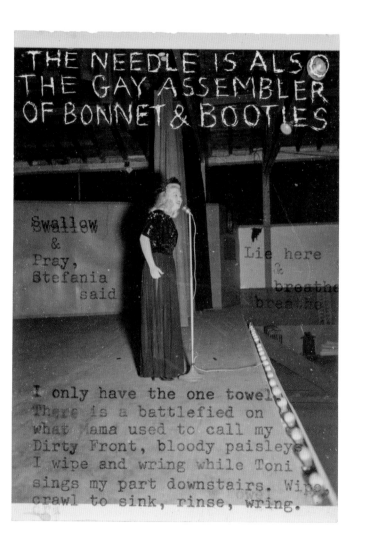

~~Stefania is not a heartless girl but~~
~~had to leave me to hemorrhage alone~~
~~after what happened to her French~~
~~counterpart in '43. (Marie-Louise-~~
~~Something-French, Maker of Angels,~~
~~Laundress, Slattern.) Not only could~~
~~Marie-Louise procure a goose in the~~
~~Occupation, dress her daughter in~~
~~a crisp pinafore, fill her son's~~
~~pockets with chocolates AND buy her-~~
~~self singing lessons, she was robbing~~
~~her country of sons which was a crime~~
~~against the State. Too few children,~~
~~too few arms, too few allies, and yet~~
~~they were sending their own Jewish~~
~~sons to~~ ~~They say her husband~~
~~turned her in because he'd been cuck-~~
~~olded, not because she was an Angel-~~
~~maker, but whatever the gossip she~~
~~was made an example of, and how. A~~
~~convincing argument for Mother⸮s~~
~~Hornet and Wren! They cropped her~~
~~hair and cut down her collar before~~
~~placing her head into the lunette~~
~~(I know you are thinking LUNETTE is~~
~~too lovely a word but the French &~~
~~the Italians can't help themselves.)~~
~~looking~~
into the bucket where her last
thoughts would land. Which is why
Stefania was so NERVOSO and ran from
my hotel with her head wrapped in
a cloak. Dear Sister, Terribly
busy, wish you were here. love, C

SOUVENIR of

Allied Officers Club

POSILLIPO ALTO, NAPLES

ĦO DAY'S COCKTAIL   L. 40

D I N N E R   L. 60

GRILLED STEAK
FRENCH FRIED POTATOES
SWEET CELLERY in Butter
===
GATEAU DIPLOMATE.

ICE CREAM.extra L.IO

     When the fever breaks
I am full of a crooked remorse
Full to the brim of the wrong rue
Remorse for the selfish living
          and I am she
     xixxfexxix sore and
     xixxfexxix free

3

You are simple as a daisy,
You are blushful as a rose,
And your little teeth are pebbles
Over which a streamlet flows.

Nothing innocent as you are
Ever under heaven did go,
Nothing, Fräulein, save your lover,
He who used to think you so.

paisley

guillotine
earring for
fashionable
ladies

Suspended in the paisley
is the teardrop & the seed

I never had a body so divine
the boys would dare not touch it

the snake

[153]

C.

after his kisses and after his slaps,
    the same chorus: look what you made me do
        look what you made me do

    our hands, our ~~nodding and shaking heads,~~
    ~~our limbs and lips~~ could form the bridge
by which we could pass over into spoken
language

you would faint if you saw the state of
~~me and my~~ things, but i am ~~alas~~ still ~~a girl~~
female, which in wartime means ~~still~~ pretty,
tho not pretty enough to reverse course. no-
one's that lovely, not even helen of T.

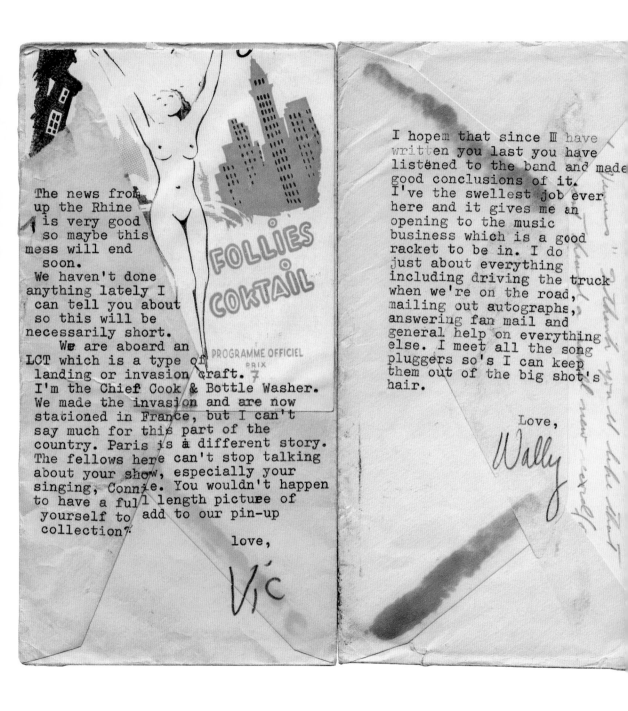

The news from
up the Rhine
is very good
so maybe this
mess will end
soon.
We haven't done
anything lately I
can tell you about
so this will be
necessarily short.
    We are aboard an
LCT which is a type of
landing or invasion craft.
I'm the Chief Cook & Bottle Washer.
We made the invasion and are now
stationed in France, but I can't
say much for this part of the
country. Paris is a different story.
The fellows here can't stop talking
about your show, especially your
singing, Connie. You wouldn't happen
to have a full length picture of
yourself to add to our pin-up
collection?

                love,

                Vic

FOLLIES
COKTAIL

PROGRAMME OFFICIEL
PRIX 7

I hopem that since III have
written you last you have
listened to the band and made
good conclusions of it.
I've the swellest job ever
here and it gives me an
opening to the music
business which is a good
racket to be in. I do
just about everything
including driving the truck
when we're on the road,
mailing out autographs,
answering fan mail and
general help on everything
else. I meet all the song
pluggers so's I can keep
them out of the big shot's
hair.

        Love,

        Wally

DEAR CONNIE   I LOST YOU
IN THE CROWD   AM LEAVING
THIS AT YR HOTEL   I HOPE
YOU DIDN'T GET TRAMPLED
I STILL WANT THAT V-DAY
SMOOCH YOU PROMISED   ME
& DO INTEND TO COLLECT ON IT

LOVE,

XOX

Well, these German girls
are still natty and sharp,
plus they speak good English.
I guess old Hitler made it
compulsory because he figured
he'd overrun England. If I
had material I could get all
kinds of suits made but it's
strictly Bring Your Own Goods
here. The married boys take
parachute silk to a hausfrau
in town and get dainties made
for their wives. The black
market is really all they
say and then some. All they
want is chocolate, soap, and
cigarettes.
Our location was
bombed to hell before
we took it over and
it's about 3/4 rubble.
We sleep four to a
room but it's a nice big room
in a swell brick building that
used to be German Officers
quarters. ha ha.

Love,

Dearest Connie,

Whether this will reach you I've no idea. I'm
here at Submarine R & R camp and am just able
to work my hand enough to write but as you can
see it looks like a child's and my apologies.
My arms and legs are badly burned but ~~hney-I--~~
honey I got off easy compared to most. Do you
remember a fellow called Sully? Good Marine
from Erie. Had a sweetheart in the USO too,
Jean I think her name was but everyone called
her Bugs. ~~Lost him on day three before the sea~~
plane showed up and tied Yours Truly to her
wing. How did they tell his mother he survived
the whole war ~~and~~ then was left out there for
the sharks. A rhetorical question. After being
torpedoed in the middle of the night, those of
us with life jackets and potato crates at sunrise
were dang sure we'd be picked up Day One. Far as
we knew the Navy was expecting us, far as we
knew, everyone was. Murder, she went down fast.
Sully and I held hands when we jumped like we
were boys on a pier. Here goes nothing, he
yelled.
He didn't even have a life jacket.
The water was blacker   than anything,
I can't describe   how black. I don't
recall any light at   all, no stars or
moon, but they   musta been there,
the planets, and   the minute we went
under I lost hold   of him, we were
slick as seals   from fuel oil.
But he had himself a   ~~se~~ crate that morning. I thought we'd made it.
Some of the men started drinking salt water that
night, and seeing things. Saw a canteen full of
spring water. Saw a beer, an oasis, Mother, and
they fought like dogs over imagined things, fought
to blood. And blood brought monsters. If you ever
cross paths with Bugs you can tell her he was
brave to the last, and he talked about her face.
He said, I like books fine but I don't remember
them the way I remember her face. All the details,
I guess he meant.
The nurse just came in with her tweezers, I'm
going to have to take a breather here and roll
over.

I.

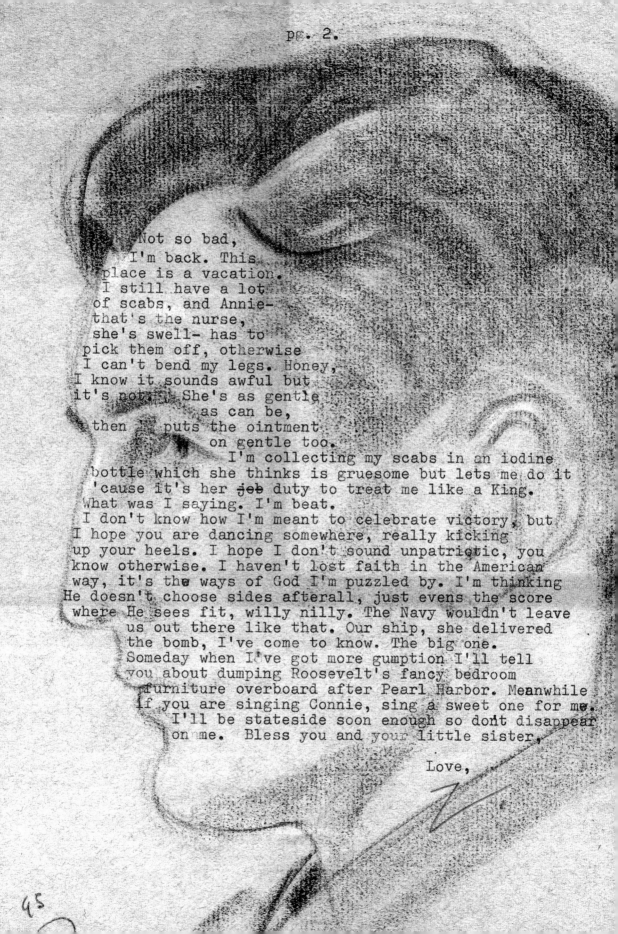

Not so bad,
I'm back. This
place is a vacation.
I still have a lot
of scabs, and Annie-
that's the nurse,
she's swell- has to
pick them off, otherwise
I can't bend my legs. Honey,
I know it sounds awful but
it's not. She's as gentle
              as can be,
  then   puts the ointment
              on gentle too.
         I'm collecting my scabs in an iodine
bottle which she thinks is gruesome but lets me do it
'cause it's her ~~job~~ duty to treat me like a King.
What was I saying. I'm beat.
I don't know how I'm meant to celebrate victory, but
I hope you are dancing somewhere, really kicking
up your heels. I hope I don't sound unpatriotic, you
know otherwise. I haven't lost faith in the American
way, it's the ways of God I'm puzzled by. I'm thinking
He doesn't choose sides afterall, just evens the score
where He sees fit, willy nilly. The Navy wouldn't leave
    us out there like that. Our ship, she delivered
    the bomb, I've come to know. The big one.
    Someday when I've got more gumption I'll tell
    you about dumping Roosevelt's fancy bedroom
      furniture overboard after Pearl Harbor. Meanwhile
    if you are singing Connie, sing a sweet one for me.
       I'll be stateside soon enough so don't disappear
       on me. Bless you and your little sister,

                    Love,

GERMAN PRISONERS

HITLERS SUPER MEN

Prisoners by the
Thousands

floating

flying

suspension   pontoon

Sister, Are we marked in some
inexplicable way? What stars did
Ma sew onto our sleeves, what
designation have they? Maybe it
is more like an odor we possess.
We are not discarded   in
this war, no, we live.   We
are not crated and   taken.
We are the   this
victors.

We do not become vapor and ash,

No, we live

GOODBY ITALY — HELLO

good trip home and +

Williamsburg Bridge, New York.

I'm Walkin' Around In A Dream

Mother Collapses After 2 Wee[ks]
Without Food on N. Y. Streets

NEW YORK, Aug. 2 (UP)—Mrs. Virginia Allen, 42, is a mother—with a capital "M."

That's why today—for the first time in two weeks—she ate a real meal and slept in a real bed.

Those two weeks mark the time since Mrs. Allen, her husband, Raymond, 45, and their three young children were evicted from their Brooklyn flat.

With $22 to their name, the home[...]

physical limits and last [...] Allen collapsed in Pro[...] Two policemen found A[...] sobbing children hoveri[...] as she lay on a stone be[...]

Malnutrition, said the [...] Kings County Hospital, [...] brought Mrs. Allen the[...]

Today, she was well [...] eat a real meal and the [...] she will recover comple[...]

Say, what abridgement have you for this evening? What masque? What music? How shall we beguile the lazy time, if not with some delight?

Sammy's Chops & Chops, Samson (The Brick) Brucks,
Proprietor. Apply to: Mr. (Uncle) Edmund (This-is-no-place
for-your-violin-sweetheart) Clark;
. . . Booker, Bookie, and Barkeep, formerly of Taxi Dance Hall,
The Frail Sister, and The Murder Room (morgue by day, jazz
by night).

employment!
dot dot dot dash !

not one of new york's finer
establishments, but it's a
joe

This city is like poetry only easier to interpret.

THE ROOSEVELT
NEW YORK

Taxicabs line up in the rain, flaunting their
yellow better than God's first canary, but I walk
across the park to meet him, full of yearning
and breathing free just as Lady Liberty bade me.
sausage, Manure, chewing gum, smoke.
The thing about Sam is he's suasive. When he
shows up I think, *Oh My, he should be locked up
somewhere,* but then he starts talking:
In his secret life he is a gatemouth and bought
an expensive trumpet and would I like a serenade?
(*I s'pose.*) Constance your beauty terrifies, and
suffering is as American as pie, and somehow he
avoided the European Theater, which means he
still believes in God, and what did we girls see
in the Italians anyway? (*Black curls, for one, prowess
in the kitchen, another.*) Have I ever tried Burlesque
? (*Of course not!!!*) because I sure have the bosom
for it, Oh don't get mad, Connie. He's so soft
he cries at the picture show and so
tough he once bit a German Shepherd in the
snout. (*I know I shouldn't, but I side with the
dog and I almost ruin the whole day.*)
I delight him with a Buck and Wing
'neath the Riverdale Arch. Come to Paris Miss
Gale, come to a costume party, come to the Ramble
Oh he makes me laugh, sis, he really does. He
kisses me under the umbrella then claims I kissed
him first. He spanks my behind and I cheerfully
call him Daddy.

honest to god Constance,
I feel like a teenager. You make
me want to check a pretty book
outa the library, you make me
want to burn my every bridge.
I've committed to memory the
sight of you gathering your wet
hair into a knot upon your head—
it was some kind of masterpiece,
the way it stayed there, and the
way it unraveled. In fact I've
memorized our room and every
second in it, just thinking of
youtaking   off your rainboots
by the   door explodes my
              heart. How I envy
              the shoe that kno
             knows your foot, &
the lucky fox that nuzzles your
throat. Songbird, I can't
promise you much but I will
promise to take care of you and
to punch anyone who harms you in
the face.   I'll be at my table
tonight relishing your every
note.

              Yours,
              Samson
PS When is your birthday? I'd
like to get you a warmer coat.

THE ROOSEVELT
New York

Unfathomable Love.

MRS. C. H. M.

MRS. C. H. MORRIS.

My Mr. Brucks took me on a Sunday drive up the Hudson. We did not hit the fawn, it was already on the road, dragging its maimed, spotted hindquarters. O look at her beseeching eyes, I cried, Stop the car! The war's ghostly children paid me a visit, as they often do, on account of those eyes-wild with fear, but with a little hope left in them. It's the hope that haunts, I've decided. Sam pulled over and I took off my espadrilles in case I needed to run for help, & took off my sweater in case I needed to stop traffic.
The fawn left a startling mahogany trail on the asphalt as she inched her way off the road. Perhaps Mother Doe beckoned from the trees. I ran off barefoot in search of a Ranger, but didn't get far before I heard the shot. I looked back and saw Sam standing over it, all business. I WAS being foolish, he was right, there was no saving to be had, his was the only mercy left. Did I really think a Park Ranger would bandage those useless legs, did I imagine a hospital for broken deer?
A bridge is a part of a gun, I found out, as Sam picked the nettles from my feet.

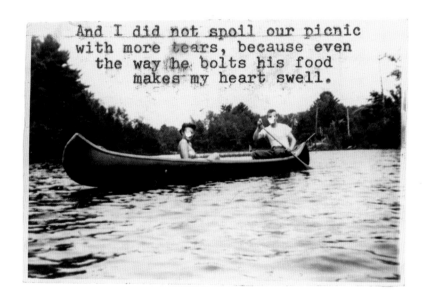

And I did not spoil our picnic
with more tears, because even
the way he bolts his food
makes my heart swell.

Smoke and mirror, cloak and dagger, sister,
secretive girl! Even in your condition, so
thin. As always, you looked like a film
star, or the center of a flower, what'sit-
called, and the boys were your handsome
petals. I wish you had joined us downtown
(a little spritz of White Shoulders in your
mouth on the train and no fiance'd be the
wiser), but I'm glad you missed my set. I
didn't sing well. It's no Copa-there are
BILLIARDS xxxxx for heaven's sake.* I could
not make myself heard over the wagering.
6666666666666666666666666666666666666666
Oh, you are clever to play "happy families"
with your fellow and move out west where
  there is no such thing as frozen. Will he
let you keep your piano? I'm afraid the only
tiny footsteps in my future will be of the
rat and roach variety. (The critters in this
building are brash. They yell back at me.)
Speaking of, Corporal Mouse has infiltrated
what's left of the Bluesbusters gang and is
temporarily sleeping on my floor. The Army
xHxxxt hasn't improved upon his charms,
  but boy-oh-boy has he ever learnt
  how to drink. As much as I'm grateful
  the war is over, I do find myself
wishing him his own WW#3--Can't
  you and your Mr. Moneybags take him with
  you, or at least put him up until he gets
  his orders? The things he says
  in his sleep are just awful.

  *a bridge is a support you make
  with your left xxxxxxxxxxxxxxxxx
  xxxxxxxxxxxxxxxxx hand while
  making a stroke with your
    right

  PS I hear MJG has set Land of
  Lost Children to music and is
  taking it on the road

GENERAL ORDERS
NUMBER   3592

AWARD OF THE BRONZE STAR MEDAL
(FIRST OAK LEAF CLUSTER)

1. TC 320. The following AWARD is announced.

RA43036765   USA

Awarded: Bronze Star Medal (First Oak Leaf Cluster) with "V" vice
action:
Theater: pub ic
Reason: in connection with military operations,   a
hostile   Sergeant First Class 🐭 distinguished
himself by   action on 22 August   while serving as
an Advisor.
                                       . On that date, Ser-
geant 🐭 , while
        on a clearing operation, came under   small arms.
                               After a short advance, the
assault   was halted despite efforts by him and
                                                    the
      body began pulling back,   wounded   ,
        trapped in a demolished house, calling for help.
Without regard for this person   , Sergeant 🐭
climbed through a window,
          and
                          the second assault began,
Sergeant 🐭 again exposed himself   in an
effort to   keep up the
momentum of the attack. When   the wounded
    fell in the open, Sergeant 🐭
                          lay down, withering ,
      to cover the evacuation of
                    his courage and
        inspiration
        alike. Sergeant First Class 🐭 's   actions
were in keeping with the hi s traditions
        and reflect   upon himself and the
military   .

Author : By   c on   n   i
            E

FOR THE COMMANDER:

OFFICIAL:

Colonel, USA
Adjutant General

Major General, USA
Chief of Staff

DISTRIBUTION:
Special

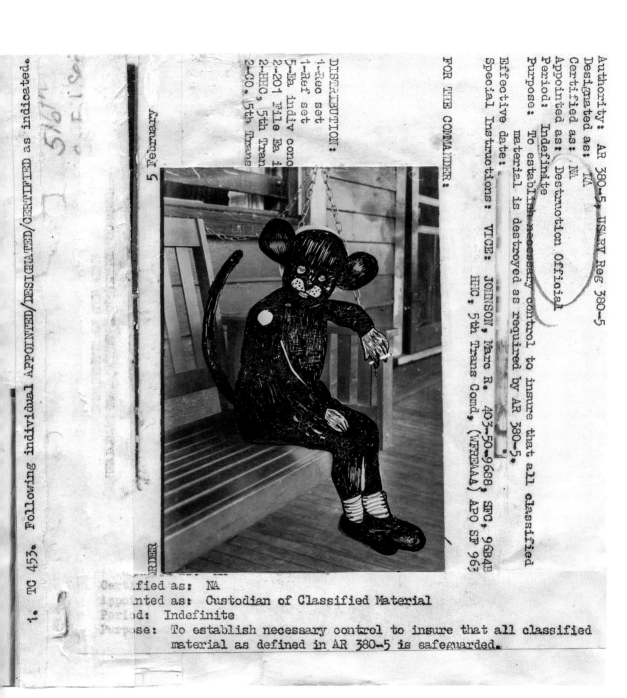

Authority: AR 380-5, USARV Reg 380-5
Designated as: NA
Certified as: NA
Appointed as: Destruction Official
Period: Indefinite
Purpose: To establish necessary control to insure that all classified
material is destroyed as required by AR 380-5.
Effective date:
Special Instructions: VICE: JOHNSON, Marc R. 403-50-9688, SFC, 96B4H
HHC, 5th Trans Comd, (WFRBAA) APO SF 963

FOR THE COMMANDER:

DISTRIBUTION:
1-Rec set
1-Ref set
5-Na Indiv conc
2-201 File Ea. i
2-HHC, 5th Tran
2-CO, 5th Trans

5 February

1. TG 453. Following individual APPOINTED/DESIGNATED/DESIGNED/CERTIFIED as indicated.

Certified as: NA
Appointed as: Custodian of Classified Material
Period: Indefinite
Purpose: To establish necessary control to insure that all classified
material as defined in AR 380-5 is safeguarded.

Therefore to us, that have taken
upon us this painful labour of
abridging, it was not easy, but
a matter of sweat
and watching.

2 Maccabees
2:26

181 He Touched Me and Made Me Stupid

A short story by Connie Gale.

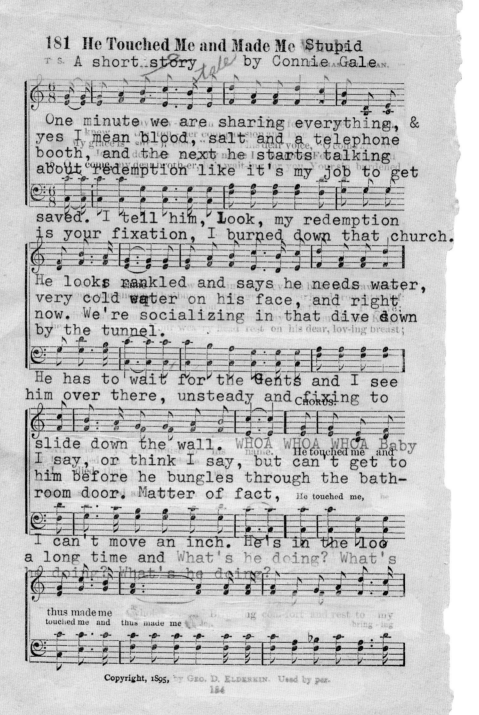

One minute we are sharing everything, &
yes I mean blood, salt and a telephone
booth, and the next he starts talking
about redemption like it's my job to get

saved. I tell him, Look, my redemption
is your fixation, I burned down that church.

He looks rankled and says he needs water,
very cold water on his face, and right
now. We're socializing in that dive down
by the tunnel.

He has to wait for the Gents and I see
him over there, unsteady and fixing to

slide down the wall. WHOA WHOA WHOA Baby
I say, or think I say, but can't get to
him before he bungles through the bath-
room door. Matter of fact,

I can't move an inch. He's in the loo
a long time and What's he doing? What's
he doing? What's he doing?

H. J. ZELLEY.   H. L. GILMOUR.

1. Have you, my dear broth-er, been res-cued from sin?
2. Are you, my dear broth-er, washed whit-er than snow?

My fox stole is all smoked up.
Sometimes I pat the little head when
I'm agitated, and am doing so now. One
of the jet beads they replaced his eyes
with has gone missing and suddenly it
strikes me as criminal I'm wearing a
murder 'round my throat. What a bad
world. When he comes back, all he says
is, I'm back. I'm watching his profile
as he relights his cigar. His one eye
has gone horizon flat, the pupil
minifying like a sunset in that blockhead
of his, and the next thing I know his
stogie's in his lap and his gabardine's
on fire. I dip the foxtail in my seltzer
and snuff it out. He's still groggy.
Run a little ice over his brow.

I'm not sure I can get him home even as
I'm suggesting it, he's awful meaty. In an
effort to revive him I whisper every
pet name I have for him into his hair:
Butch, Grizzly, Doc. He orders three
black coffees from the waitress,"and
step on it," which brings him round some,
but now I'm so tired I can only think
about the bed at his place, which is so
superior to mine--mine you have to
climb a ladder to 'cause it's over the
kitchenette--plus I'm fretting he might
reignite. The smoked, wet animal
around my neck is making me nauseous.

Sam honey, let's vamoose.

NOTICE!
TO OUR GUESTS

Tuesday May 30th is a Legal Holiday.

All bars will be closed for the day.

"YOU KNOCK MY SOCKS OFF, CONNIE G."

All the pretty brunettes knocked his
socks off, I came to find out, but
by then I was deep in the weeds. He
made me laugh and had an appetite
for and an understanding of what was
eating at me and I never was a girl
afraid of needles.

Don't Forget To Call The Desk
To Get Your Liquors And Beer
Before Midnight Tonight.

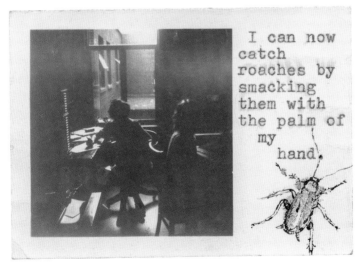

I can now catch roaches by smacking them with the palm of my hand.

I wear my dress with the beaded
collar, I thought I looked nice
but maybe not, he gives me none
of the usual compliments. Brucks
isn't drinking and it's his first
night on the wagon; he regretfully
orders an iced tea. Woe is he.
I am aware there is no part of me
that hasn't lost luster but I need
him to renew my contract. He says
that's Uncle Ed's domain. He says,
Alas, everything that comforts us
can be lost to us, I should know
that from the war.

POEMS INTENDED TO INCITE THE
    UTMOST DEPRESSION

It wasn't so long ago I pulled up
my dress in midtown to show him my
fanciful stockings and garters and
he prettynear passed out, but tonight
my hands shake lifting my wine, the
stem of the glass seems brittle as
an icicle, I'm afraid of snapping it.
He's got that grim look which means
he's about to get amnesic about
promises. I tell him, Honey I'm in
a spot of trouble.
It's dawning on me Sis, that life may
not be long enough to learn my lesson
in. How do you find California??

Congratulations

Dear Sister,

~~I've fallen pregnant (again), another odd expression, with an excuse and an accident built into it.~~ Thank you for sending the photo of you and your little girl. ~~I've fallen (again), pregnant.~~ I see you left the maternity ward with your 20 inch waist restored! Sam and I are pettifogging, no hope of a honeymoon stage, much less a honeymoon. ~~Recently I found out he's 1) Married 2) Catholic.~~ He doesn't want me anywhere near Chops-n-Chops anymore, onstage or otherwise, ~~says I'm "showing" and showing spoils the show.~~ We had a big row about it ~~and now I have a black eye and broke toes. (No more dancing for you, he said, and he kissed my toes through my hose before he broke them.)~~ ~~I'm too embarrassed to admit I thought he loved me so I won't.~~ All my love to you, Sis. I've fallen ~~(is the story)~~ and went whimpering to Uncle ED, who knows what a pill Sam can be and took me in. Ed's older than Pa, twice as queer, & illiterate but is kind to me so far. Congratulations on your bundle of joy!

and telegraphing to find out. This last time I called both San Francis

and Atlanta and didn't get in touch   until two in the morning.

        Well, C , that's about all for this time. I'll try to write
again soon.

P.S. The New address is

It's a Boy,

They come when they want to, don't they just. Why didn't
you warn me? I thought I could do it on my own, in the room behind
the kitchen, formerly the pantry, which Ed calls the Music Room
because he doesn't like it when I sleep there. Contents therein:
Army cot, a quilt in a loud chrysanthemum pattern, violin, sheet
music, my diaries, sepia and best pen, the Olympia and my letters.
(Yours I keep separate and tied with a bit of floss.) Oh, and some
playing cards and an unlucky German's flask.
        The pains came first thing in the morning, promptly activat
a bygone injury, breaking afresh the already broken, and after a
whole day of it I was begging Ed for a needle. The noises I made
scared the scruples right out of him. After that I started chanting
like a monk (Sol-ve polluti, La-bii reatum), I was too weak to
scream. We didn't know how much blood was too much blood, so Ed
kept checking the sheets. I noticed he had what we used to call
a "full salute of his silent flute" when he rolled me over, pushing
and kneading my backside. O Sis, he's decrepit but his nethereye
snaps to attention at the most preposterous moments. Get ye to the
tiled floor, Constance. I spent a number of hours in the loo,
haggling with the spirits, pledging my return to the church, any
church. Still I refused the hospital. Whose name would I give them,
for example? ED said, Christallmighty, tell them Clark Clark Clark,
I will make you an Honest Connie & no more of this Unclepiffle,
to which I said, Let me die in the tub (an option he considered but
worried aloud how he would 'splain away the bruises in my arm's
crook and elsewhere, they might throw him in the joint), so
I relented and let him shove me into a cab, unaccompanied.
        The Methodist Hosp. claims to welcome Jew and Gentile,
Protestant and Catholic, heathen and infidel, but I wore out my
welcome right away. They wheeled me to the Bead Nurse, whose job
it is to make mother and babe their matching bracelets. I told
her Gale and Clark, Brucks and Doe. The pain took my wits from me.
Who are you? I don't know. Who gave you the shot? A stranger on 6th
Street. How did you get those sores? I don't remember. I lost my
purse. He died in the war. Please get it out of me. Maybe I called
the baby an It, maybe I said I don't want it, which I didn't mean,
but whatever I said made them call the authorities and when they
took him from me they did not bring him back.

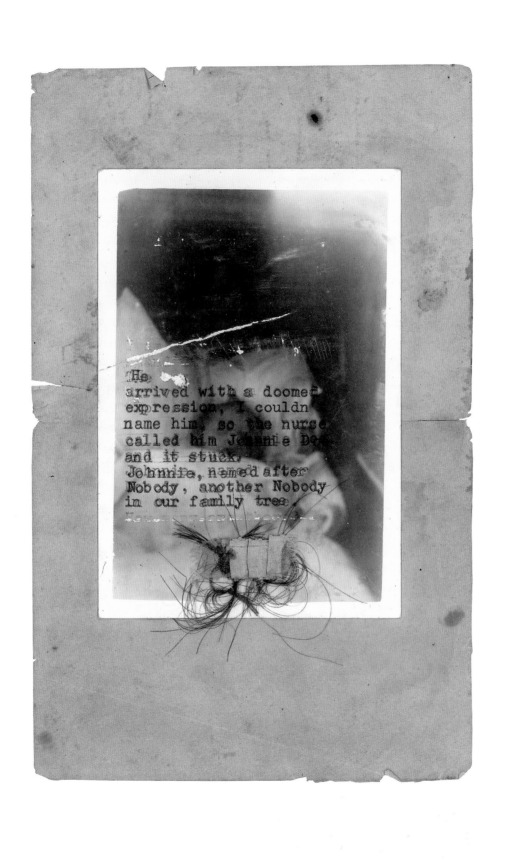

He
arrived with a doomed
expression, I couldn't
name him, so the nurse
called him Johnnie Doe
and it stuck.
Johnnie, named after
Nobody, another Nobody
in our family tree.

PUT THE HEAT TO HIROHITO

NEVER MIND THIS

MY ONE AND ONLY SISTER WHY HAVE
YOU FORSAKEN AND ETCETERA,
    Maybe if I just send pictures they won't
be confiscated? I am still awaiting a
court date and a response from you if it's not
too much trouble. Uncl Ed is doing his best
to get me out of here.
I've run out of paper again and got into

trouble trying to trade for a few sheets so

have resorted to typing over these, I hope
they are legible. Why I've held onto them I

do not know, can't recollect which face goes

with what name   whose with what

    THEY'VE GIVEN ME SOMETHING TO HELP MY SLEEP
WHICH CLOUDS MY THOUGHTS AND DOESNT HELP MY
TYPING EITHER, IT'S JUST A CASE OF NERVES
I*AM*SOR ANYONE WOULD BE NERVOUS HERE.
    HAVE SLEPT WITHOUT THE DREAMS COMING SO
THAT'S SOMETHING. DO YOU STILL HAVE NIGHTMARES
DO YOU STILL SING IN YOUR SLEEP. ONE TIME
YOU WHISTLED.
        WOULD give anything to bitean apple
smell the ocean see you

                    love, connie

PS Can only use the typing machine one hr
per day so pls forgive mistakes and typos

THE YOUNG MEN'S CHRISTIAN ASSOCIATIONS • THE NATIONAL CATHOLIC COMMUNITY SERVICE
THE SALVATION ARMY • THE YOUNG WOMEN'S CHRISTIAN ASSOCIATIONS
THE JEWISH WELFARE BOARD • THE NATIONAL TRAVELLERS AID ASSOCIATION

COPYRIGHT 1942 BY PORTO-SERVER · CHICAGO

JOLLY ROGERS

BEST DAMN HEAVY BOMB GROUP IN THE WORLD

Dear Long Lost,
I have no good news.
I wonder how you and your daughter are. Is it
true the folks took the train out west to help
with the diapering and swaddling? I remember
how much Pa professed to love babies because
they couldn't smart-aleck him. I hope he will
be decent to your girl when she grows, and not
assign her Cinderella chores, like picking up
rotten plums with her bare hands or scraping
paint off the banister with mirror shards—
remember that one? How furious we were out
there in the sun and then you got the
heat stroke. THAT SHOWED HIM!
Which do you think would be more shameful for
Mama and Pa, prison or the loony bin? It appears
my fate is still ~~undecided~~ undetermined. Which
would be more shameful for you? Mouse I don't give
a rat's ass about as far as his opinion goes.

    As ever,
    Constance

Dear, About

100 years ago there was a madman in a French

better at Walnut Point I will I

asylum who doctors paid to fornicate with their

was going through boat cause the

dead lady patients--the article didn't say WHY, it

food was sure terrible and the

just described the physicians yukking it up. They

place here is O.K.

paid the man in hot coffee or tea, which was fine

with him until they brought him a lady who'd been

I saw the Robert E Lee going up

guillotined (she hadn't murdered anyone, the

the bay the other day and it is a

guillotine had just been invented and they needed

good size boat.

to test its effectiveness) and he simply refused

to do their bidding for any amount of cafe au lait.

Well I said about enough of

Let's play the old game:

myself. How is everything going

WHO IS MAD?

with you and the family? I hope

☐ ME

☐ THE DOCTORS

to be home for Easter Sunday and

Sometimes the doctors open someone up and say, Nevermind.
Does God? What I mean is, are there some people who--
when God takes stock of their souls--are just hopeless?

② but I won't say that I won't quit. I'll never drink anymore,

She .... she
was ....
is we .... ak
new ....
get .... the
trouble. We sure had fun
though. As for me, I got lucky.
a ....
guess .... just
she .... cause
have .... Then, I'll try -
get you .... to write to.
.... my new Id
shade of nail polish - the color

CAN A WOMAN IN AMERICA STEP OFF
THE EDGE OF THE WORLD AND NEVER BE
MISSED???

It has been almost a year since
police picked up Jane D. who was
wandering aimlessly round this
city and she hasnt spoken one word
or more precisely she did say "OH"
when an orderly (accidentally?)
stepped on her slippered foot. Even
under what they call the Truth Serum
drugs and electric shock treatments*
she maintains a stony silence. She
is known on the ward as "that piece
of furniture".

XXX
XXX As for me, I got lucky.

They brought me the baby whose
name is John and are ~~releasing me~~
letting me go home tomorrow- at this
juncture Home is Uncle Ed's but I
do feel if Sam could just see Johnnie
and how dear he is, maybe
                              just maybe -

*In Italy electric shock
was used to render pigs
comatose before they
became pancetta

..... wearing
a bright red sweater - brown
myself. I haven't been out .....
girl since I left Atlantic City.
The only way I have any fun

After I was discharged and got Johnnie
back. I arranged to meet Sam at the
                  diner, thinking the babe
          might tenderize the brute.
                He was still wee enough
                to be swaddled and I lay
                him there beside me
          in   the booth while I
        applied colors to my face.
            Brucka   was lat   he's
                always la   late.
When   he saw I'd   brought
Johnnie   along, he turned
purple, so I excused   myself.
He followed me into the Ladies
and asked   Why didn't I just
give it   up, he already had
a family,   JesusChristConnie,
and What was I doing shacking up
with   Uncle Ed. He could not
        put his hands round a stem
so small so he used the washroom towels, yanking them from the metal dis-
penser, veins in his forearms swell-
ing (he used to box). I remember a
pale blue stripe. The towels were in
a loop, like prison escape sheets in
miniature, the pattern repeating
itself into infinity. When he had a
meter's worth, he ripped a length off,
starting the tear with his teeth. Good
strong teeth Sam has. I just stood by
and I'm going to hell   for it

After ~~he~~ it was done,
Sam handed him back to
me, Here you go,
Mother.
What was I to do
but bring him to
Uncle Ed?

"godammit connie "

"I saved you
from that Brucks
& nearly went to
jail on account
of you being so
Stupit to bring
it Home I had
to Dump It in
the Bin & Now
we have to
Leave Town
cause if authoretie
athroroties find
out What Really
Happened it will
be Hare to Belive
plus Your
All Cracked Up
again "

You're naturally funny,
Uncle Ed Says, Stop
playing the blues. The violin
can also fiddle. Oh what he
calls his "appetites" and how
they dampen mine. There is a
sleeping bag of snow since I last checked in,
an aggressive opacity through the single
pain pane. He claims there is no snow, it is not
winter, but I am sick again, of
course it snows and snow it must.
Butterscotch in my hankie, butterscotch
and blood. I've stopped washing my hair
so as not to see the dark beasts dancing
at the drain. I should be good by now at
leaving well enough alone. Talcum and
confectioners. Fluttering gnats of
ice. My sweat smells like
house paint. In between alive and
not so. Sister, it smarts. Build me
a bridge of silver and send me on
my way.

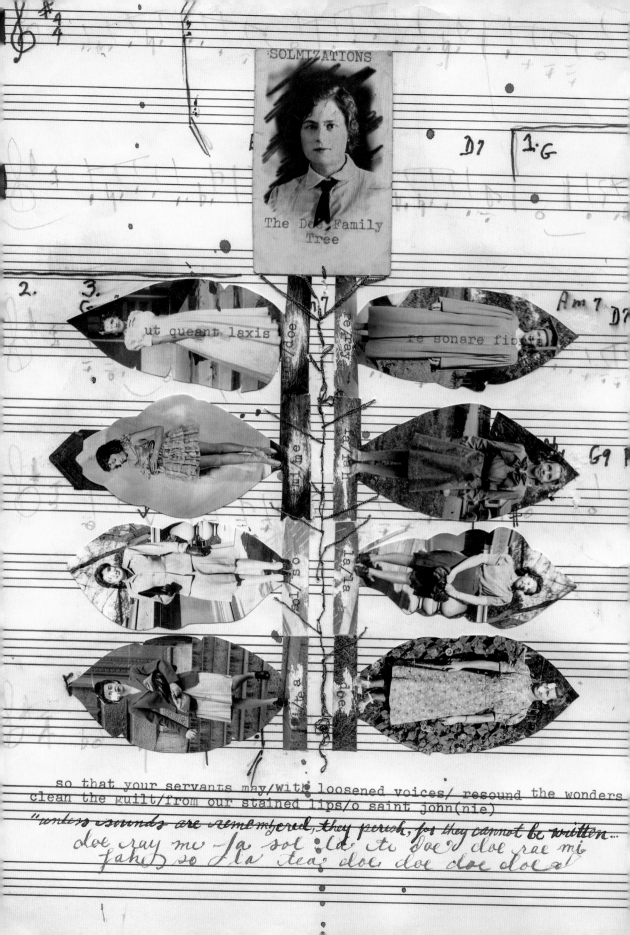

SOLMIZATIONS

The Doe Family Tree

ut queant laxis

re sonare fibris

so that your servants may/with loosened voices/ resound the wonders
clean the guilt/from our stained lips/o saint john(nie)

"unless sounds are remembered, they perish, for they cannot be written...
doe ray me — fa sol : la ti doe doe rae mi
fah; so fla tea; doe doe doe doe ⌐

The police bought Ed's story about finding Johnnie
in the bin, so they let him go and put me in.

Somebody Somebody, Esq. gave me a talking-to about
how to show remorse in a court of law, but as you
know I'm more the frozen type.

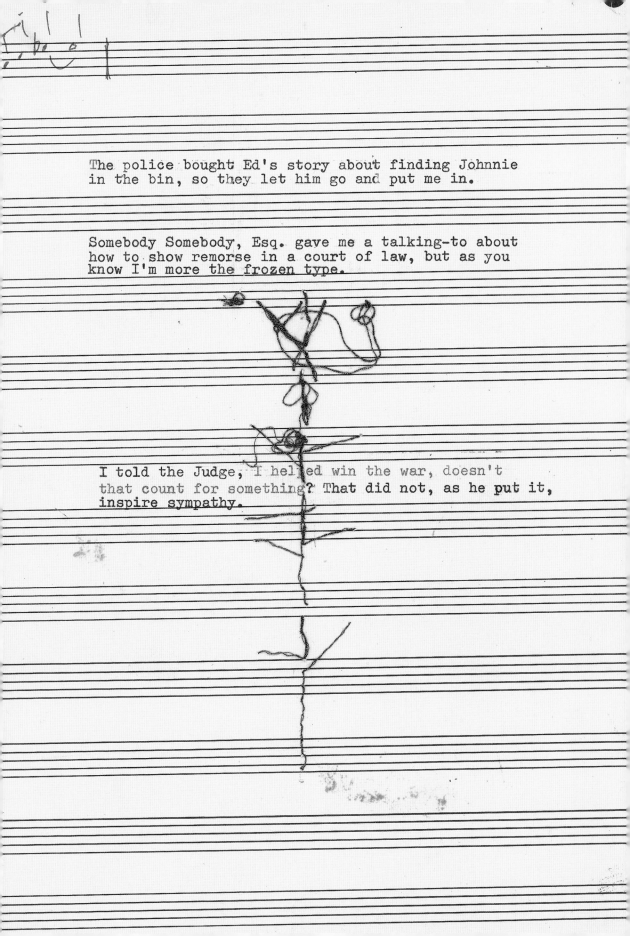

I told the Judge, I helped win the war, doesn't
that count for something? That did not, as he put it,
inspire sympathy.

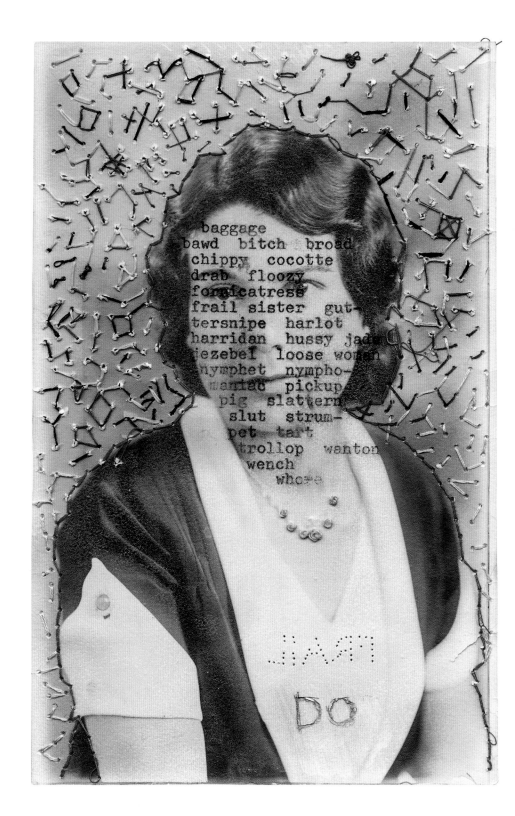

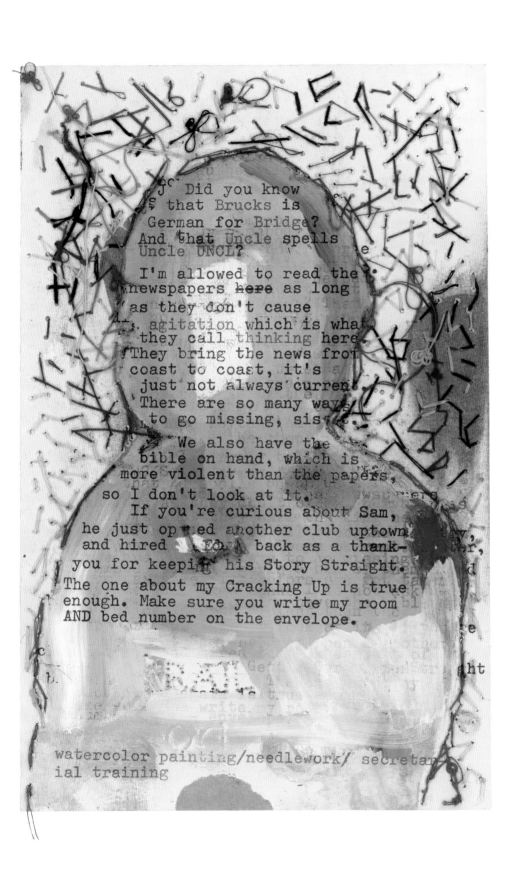

Did you know
that Brucks is
German for Bridge?
And that Uncle spells
Uncle UNCL?

I'm allowed to read the
newspapers ~~here~~ as long
as they don't cause
agitation which is what
they call thinking here.
They bring the news from
coast to coast, it's
just not always current.
There are so many ways
to go missing, sister.

We also have the
bible on hand, which is
more violent than the papers,
so I don't look at it.
If you're curious about Sam,
he just opened another club uptown,
and hired Ed back as a thank-
you for keeping his Story Straight.
The one about my Cracking Up is true
enough. Make sure you write my room
AND bed number on the envelope.

watercolor painting/needlework/ secretar
ial training

the trouble is between us Every thing was going
perfect as far as I was concerned but it
looked different on your part. I will close now
for I do not want to make things worse than
they are now Please write soon and let me
know just what the trouble is

Dear Little Johnnie,

P.S.

am no

When your daddy asked why I was so fond
of the Italians, I didn't give him the
whole list. Once upon a time, your mother
was a bluesbuster and we do-si-doed up
Italy's crooked spine. It was always too
hot or too cold there. We sang on a plat-
form with a canvas top while the soldiers
got drenched in warm rain. I played
Paganini & Shostakovich in a blizzard,
wearing a gown and fingerless gloves. We
slept in tents in an olive grove, with
skins of wine hanging from the branches,
we slept in a palace whose walls were
papered in butter-colored silk. We had
mass in a field, we had mass in rubble, we
had mass in a cathedral and its cherubs
were our sky. A mine blew mud out of a
ditch and it landed in my eye. And Oh, the
hue of the Tyrrhenian, Johnnie, & moun-
tains spitting fire, and pasta sculpted
into ears or shells. Luigi sliced raw
octopus so thinly it looked like the
ruffled petals of a bearded iris on my
plate, & his hair smelled of oregano.
Hunger is my excuse for my sin. The nuns
soaked lemons in birdbaths to make per-
fume and the monks massaged wild roses in
sugar, then made a jam of it.

        every hour i spend in this place
     i get closer to you johnnie by
        getting more see- through, every
     day i grow backwards & fade.
     you may not believe this, but onceupona
time i was a child feigning sleep. i was
a girl.

You know I'm only fooling.

Dear Little Sister,

When you asked why I liked the Italians
so much, I didn't answer you the whole
story. Luigi said, The nuns and monks, they
can't make love so they infuse their recipes
with frustrazione.   In Naples, there were
often animal noises coming from an army
truck parked on a side street, a local boy
hawking the wares. "You wanna jig/My sister
is clean." I should be ashamed to admit I
was already versed in those sounds, by then
I knew that carnal music well. If a Yank
caught The Disease he faced charges for a
self-inflicted wound, but once the sister
was worn out, it was typical to send the
delinquent girl to il manicomio. Hunger is
a good excuse for most every sin. Once upon
a time we were girls who stayed up late to
share our secrets, feigning sleep at the
coming of papa's boots. You covered your
mouth with your hand so he wouldn't catch
you smiling. This secret is not about Little
Johnnie, it's the other Nobody Doe on my
mind today, who was very likely a Nessuno
il Daino if you catch my drift. Sarge slapped
me for a few reasons—he'd been wary since the
mozzarella and songbird supper, but I had
never even heard of oregano and I liked the
smell of it very much. Honestly, I liked Luigi
very much but thesituatione was impossibile.
When he dipped his finger in the
Marmellata di Rose, I swooned, and for
swooning paid the piper.
After the angelmaker
left, toni came to my room and rinsed the blood
from my towel. i think it's letting up, she said, but you
are like chalk and your hair is soaked. she invented a
lullaby and drew something on my back with a shaky
finger, letters or symbols, not a swastika a solmization
of sorts. i had the goose flesh, i felt her write
shivers, and all the while she sang nonsense about
roses and lemons and a kinder god.

DEAR SIS,

The mystery of
J. Doe's un-
identified corpse
remains unsolved
today as the
Coroner's office found no hints
from the autopsy. Well I'm
sure sorry to be so macabre
but you don't know what it's
like in here. The corpse was
wearing black mesh stockings
when the hunters found her
            in a partly "mummified"
state. They love to say the word
NUDE over and over in these reports,
as in NUDE, NUDE,PARTIALLY NUDE.
    Aside from the hose, she was
    nude. Another Jane was found
    on Broadway sitting in the
    middle of the street,
    partially nude, before
        being committed to
        the State Hosp,
        pls write bk,
            as ever,

rae
ray

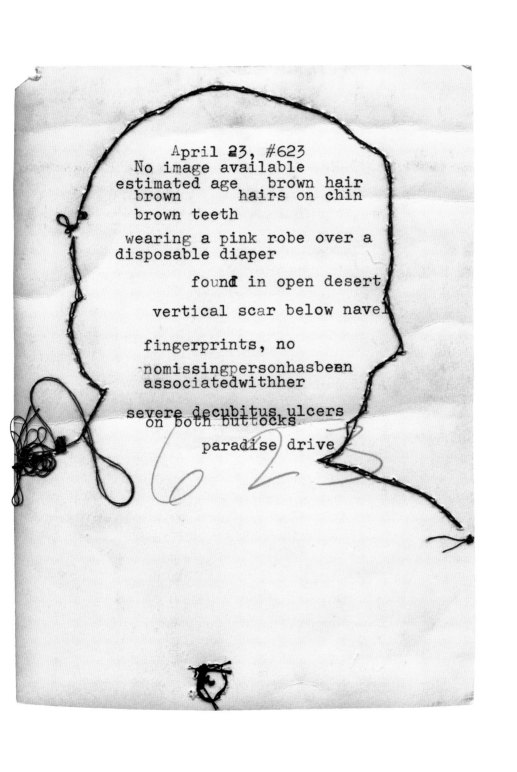

April 23, #623
No image available
estimated age   brown hair
brown   hairs on chin
brown teeth

wearing a pink robe over a
disposable diaper

        found in open desert

    vertical scar below navel

    fingerprints, no

    nomissingpersonhasbeen
    associatedwithher

    severe decubitus ulcers
        on both buttocks

        paradise drive

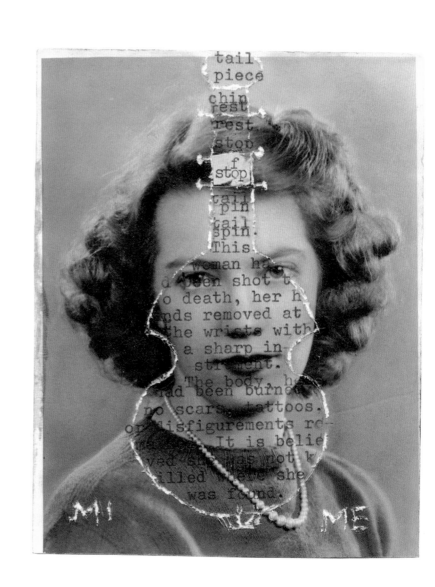

tail
piece
chin
rest
rest
stop
f
stop
tail
pin
tail
spin.
This
woman ha
d been shot t
o death, her h
nds removed at
the wrists with
a sharp in
strument.
The body h
ad been burne
no scars, tattoos,
or disfigurements re
It is belie
ved she was not k
illed where she
was found.

MI   ME

Dear Sis,

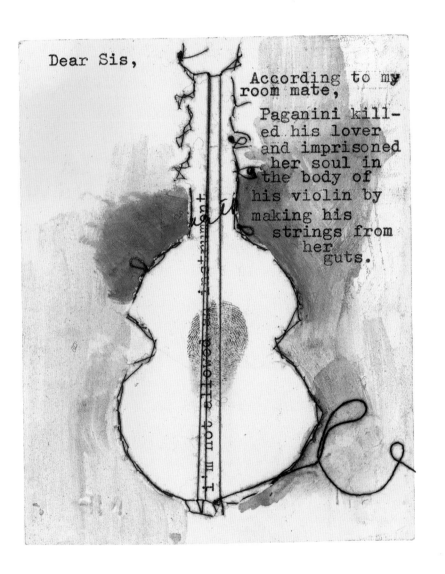

According to my room mate,

Paganini kill-ed his lover and imprisoned her soul in the body of his violin by making his strings from her guts.

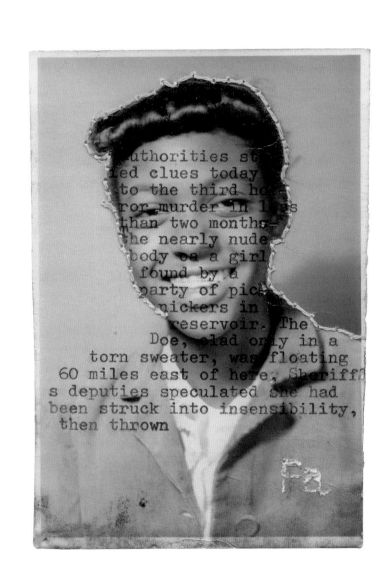

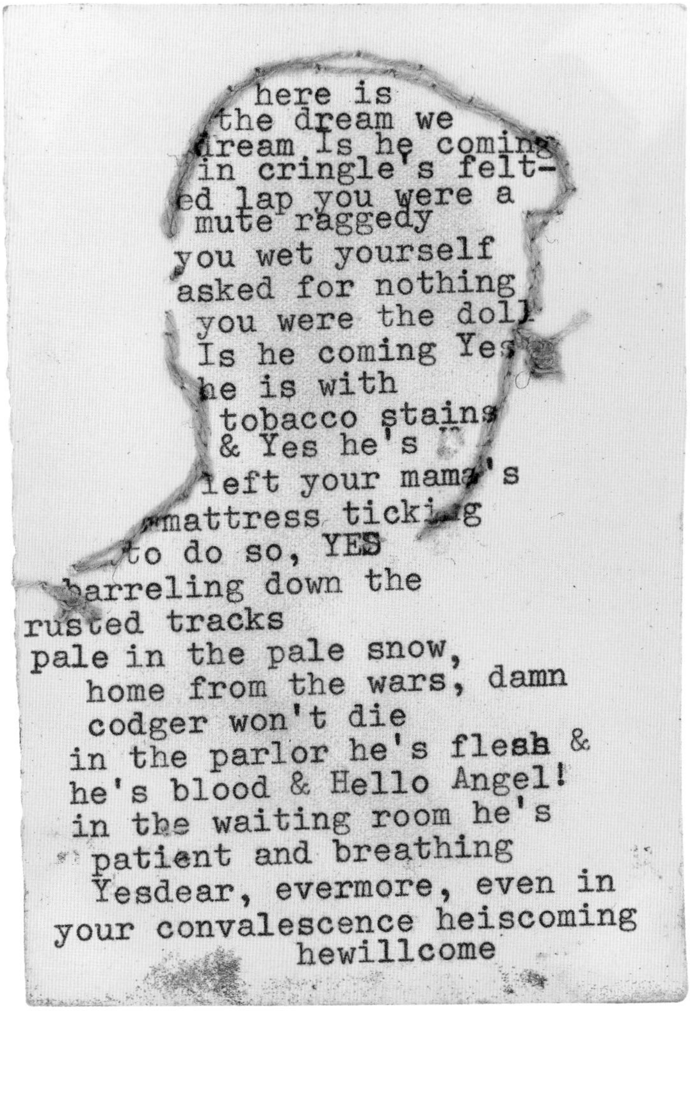

here is
the dream we
dream Is he coming
in cringle's felt-
ed lap you were a
mute raggedy
you wet yourself
asked for nothing
you were the doll
Is he coming Yes
he is with
tobacco stains
& Yes he's
left your mama's
mattress ticking
to do so, YES
barreling down the
rusted tracks
pale in the pale snow,
home from the wars, damn
codger won't die
in the parlor he's flesh &
he's blood & Hello Angel!
in the waiting room he's
patient and breathing
Yesdear, evermore, even in
your convalescence heiscoming
hewillcome

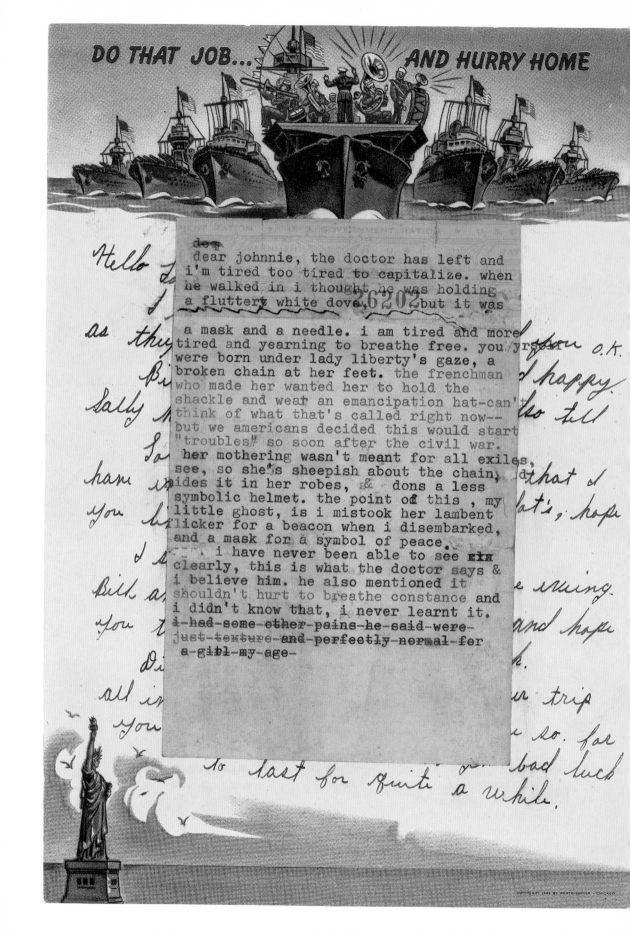

dear johnnie, the doctor has left and
i'm tired too tired to capitalize. when
he walked in i thought he was holding
a fluttery white dove but it was

a mask and a needle. i am tired and more
tired and yearning to breathe free. you
were born under lady liberty's gaze, a
broken chain at her feet. the frenchman
who made her wanted her to hold the
shackle and wear an emancipation hat-can't
think of what that's called right now--
but we americans decided this would start
"troubles" so soon after the civil war.
her mothering wasn't meant for all exiles,
see, so she's sheepish about the chain,
hides it in her robes, & dons a less
symbolic helmet. the point of this , my
little ghost, is i mistook her lambent
flicker for a beacon when i disembarked,
and a mask for a symbol of peace.
i have never been able to see
clearly, this is what the doctor says &
i believe him. he also mentioned it
shouldn't hurt to breathe constance and
i didn't know that, i never learnt it.
i-had-some-other-pains-he-said-were-
just-texture-and-perfectly-normal-for
a-girl-my-age-

Jan 6 1943
New River N.C.

UNITED STATES MARINES

Dear Sister,
Sam said, Forget about bloody Italy. At
the Roosevelt, we invented a holiday called Naughty Sunday, and everything was
allowed--Chesterfields in bed, real maple
syrup, uncombed hair. Jumping in fountains,
bruised hipbones, and Johnnie Doe. I mean
the notion of a little Johnnie, his
twinkle and promise. Sam would read Poe
aloud, his glasses gullying the bridge*
of his nose, while I ate bear claws beside him. If Johnnie had lived long
enough to be a real boy and I a real Ma,
I would've read him stories about animals-
habits of the giant mottled eel, handsome
foxes sunning themselves, rabbits that
scream like children after too much cake,
& the cuttlefish-oddest beastie of all-
who besides making the sepia ink and
black spaghetti, hunt from the minute they
hatch & will eat their own siblings if
necessary. Mama Cuttle dies soon after
she lays her eggs so she doesn't witness
the cannibalism of her offspring** Where
the Papa Squid fits in I haven't been able
to parse from the magazine donations here.
By the way, Papa sent a postcard, so did
Mouse. I dont mind being disowned, not
really. The doctor says though my
Troubling Mentality continues,
AGAINSTHISBETTERJUDGEMENT he's releasing
me to Ed's custody. I said, Oh who cares,
but between you and me Who Cares is a
question I'd like answered.

*did i already mention Brucks is German
for bridge? a bridge is the upper, bony
part of the nose, but also the curvy bit
of a pair of specs that rests on the nose,
so Sam had a bridge atop a bridge atop a bridge.

**some mothers PREFER to outlive their children-
ours may be one of those

HOME

I smiled at a baby from the porch
today and the babe smiled back.
I leaned over the bannister to
goo-goo-ga at the creature,
resurrecting some old self of mine.
The child's mama wasnt scared of me
either, but now that toothless smile
feels like a punch. I'd rather not
have feelings, can't find slumber
alongside them, and that's why Uncl
Ed's okay by me- always yammering
about numb-this and numb-that, how
he was made and born numb and never
needed help to get there, far as I
know. Funny thing is, he's fretful
about it. Lots of feelings about
how he can't feel, which I mostly
don't mind him repeating.

        in the house on diamond alley,
we warmed each other, you and me,
  warmed each other too,   and
      i was the ~~bigger~~, iwas your
        shawl and your shade wasn't i

Twilight

...is dreaded
...ly some of us
because of what it
means:HERE COMES THE
NIGHT. A bus is breaki g
down outside, the wind's
up, a storm's coming. I
eckoned after 3 swigs and
a game of solitaire I coul
turn this night off, but th
Unanswerables show up and
start in on me like a swar
of bees: What's the diffe
ence between this room
and a locked one? Is th t
sadsack love the las
love I'll ever
make?Flyingbridg
or fire escape? I smel Ed in the
kitchen, boiling a tongue for supper
even though he knows I can't swallow,
a flyswatter or spatula tucked into his belt,
mutbering. Since Johnnie Doe, Ed's temper is
a canopy fire, quicker and hotter. I saved you,
he keeps reminding me, You owe me, make nice.
Why do I itch so? This blanket is so cheap, it
squeaks. Since Johnnie, the xmas tree's still
p. Since Johnnie, we use his leftover diapers
or my headaches, fill them with ice. His play-
pen's filled with emp bottles. Since Johnnie,
Ed no longer circumven my face, since Johnnie
a closed fist.   I'm halfway to the
fire escape when comes cocksure pounding on
the door. 'Course I don't answer, not allowed.

Orange,
New Jersey:
The body of an
attractive
woman, her
skull and jaw
fractured, was found
on the Passaic River
bank by two fish-
ermen yesterday.
Her age was esti-
mated at 25. Police
believe the Jane
Doe, who wore a
fur-trimmed black
coat and one suede shoe
was a victim of a mur-
der and may have been
swept up by the river
from a point upstream.
An autopsy disclosed
that the girl was
alive when she
entered the
water.

dec 8,
red or auburn,
age and weight
unknown, bobby
pins & a hair
net, light peach
slip by Blanche,
some sources say
light blue,
liquid stockings,
golden crowns,

had given birth
to at least one

child, copy of dated
Brooklyn Eagle
in homemade
casket, glued
and nailed,
dirt and rocks
weighted and

submerged

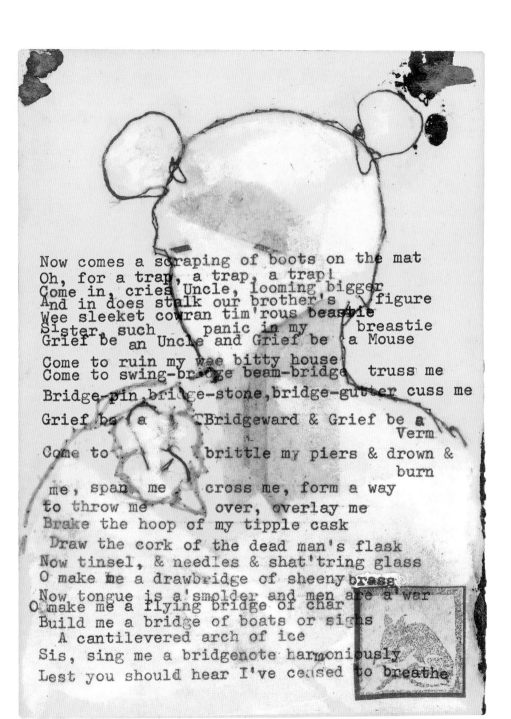

Now comes a scraping of boots on the mat
Oh, for a trap, a trap, a trap!
Come in, cries Uncle, looming bigger
And in does stalk our brother's figure
Wee sleeket cowran tim'rous beastie
Sister, such panic in my breastie
Grief be an Uncle and Grief be a Mouse

Come to ruin my wee bitty house
Come to swing-bridge beam-bridge truss me

Bridge-pin,bridge-stone,bridge-gutter cuss me

Grief be a Bridgeward & Grief be a
Verm

Come to brittle my piers & drown &
burn

me, span me cross me, form a way
to throw me over, overlay me
Brake the hoop of my tipple cask
Draw the cork of the dead man's flask
Now tinsel, & needles & shat'tring glass
O make me a drawbridge of sheeny brass
Now tongue is a'smolder and men are a'war
O make me a flying bridge of char
Build me a bridge of boats or sighs
A cantilevered arch of ice
Sis, sing me a bridgenote harmoniously
Lest you should hear I've ceased to breathe

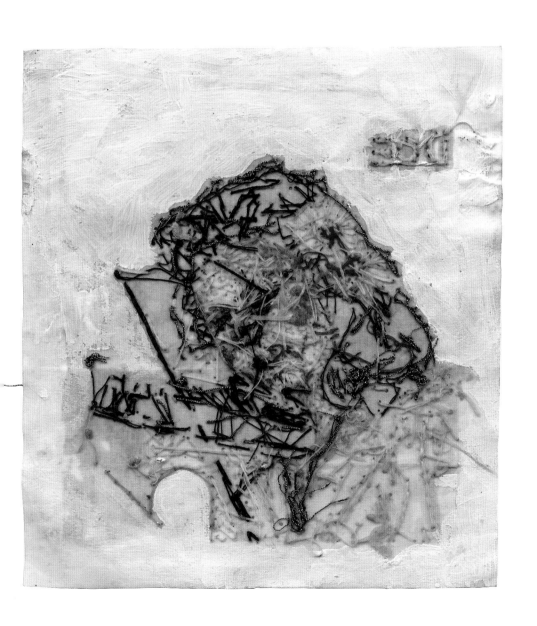